July 10, 19°

Dear Rena,
I hope you enjoy
my book.
Lots of luck to you!
Love,
Trudy

Dedication

In loving memory of Belle Halpern Goldberg,
who listened and responded,
and listened, and listened…

May this life bring you all the happiness you can stand and only enough sorrow to show you the difference.

...from Aunt Lucy's autograph book

1   *Ruth*

I was young and in love in Jerusalem, and, although my future, academically and professionally, was somewhat unclearly laid out before me, I felt content. It was the spring of 1979. All was well with the world — my world, anyway. If time could have stood still, life for me would have remained blissfully filled with romance, poetry, nature's beauty, and the profundity of my people's history. I had only to glance in the mirror or into the eyes of nearly any of the city's numerous female students to be filled with confidence that my status as heart-throb would endure as long as the pinkish stones of the city I loved. A native Israeli, I was twenty-seven and well built. I had thick, dark, curly hair with matching eyebrows and mustache, deep-set gray eyes, and well-proportioned features, if one can be objective about such things. I suppose one has to be in order to come to grips with a very important aspect of one's identity. I don't believe I was ever conceited or arrogant, but the fact is I was not awfully hard to look at.

At this point in my life I had been living for several months with an Israeli girlfriend, Ruth. Being in love with her heightened my sensual awareness of the flavor and mystery of Jerusalem. I had always loved to be in love in that city. The experience was not quite the same anywhere else.

Ruth was not my first love, though I was hers. She and I had many good times together. We used to hike early in the morning in the Judaean Mountains and watch the sun rise as we breathed in the special aroma of the trees and the damp earth. We would walk for hours through Jerusalem's Old City.

On one of our last nights together we stood on the Mount of Olives, overlooking Mt. Moriah and the heart of the city. I can still feel the wind blowing. There was something about the sound and the feel of the wind in a quiet place that imparted to me a deeply spiritual feeling. The historical character of the site gave me a strange, almost eerie perspective on life. And, of course, sharing these feelings with Ruth filled my romantic soul with joy.

She brought me much pleasure in many ways. Ruth was a sweet, lovely girl, whom I admired for her modest, gentle, unassuming demeanor. She was marvelously talented at Israeli folk dancing, and I used to enjoy immeasurably watching her, with other students, gracefully execute all the lively movements characteristic of Israeli dance.

A student of literature, Ruth was exceedingly fond of poetry. We would spend hours reading it together and thus would share our most intimate feelings.

I'm afraid that the poignant memories I have of this relationship are not accompanied by any feelings of great pride in myself. One would have to be very lenient in judging that I was merely inconsiderate and ungentlemanly. It pains me to think of how I must have hurt her and, almost as much, to reflect on how callous a person I must have been.

Ruth was a virgin when we first met, a sensitive, thoughtful girl of twenty-two. Though what lovemaking we did was delightful for both of us, I soon found the incompleteness of it to be thoroughly frustrating. She was very reluctant to engage in that one act that would have brought me the release I longed for. I grew to have very little patience with her slowness.

One day she yielded to me. While I doubt that she regretted her decision, she surely did not enter into the experience casually, nor did her subsequent lovemaking lack personal depth and commitment.

Like many another Jerusalem student facing the rapidly approaching summer, I was eager to get myself some remunerative work, preferably work which would fit in well with my classes. I was thrilled when an interview at the university landed me a full year's job as one of several resident advisers to few hundred American students in one of its dormitories.

However, my gratification at being hired dimmed by comparison to the elation I experienced once I had actually commenced working. It's curious how the pitfalls intrinsic to a set of circumstances can be so effectively disguised as to convince the victim-to-be that his life is at its rosiest and that its being so is caused precisely by these circumstances.

My responsibilities consisted of familiarizing the students with the city and even the whole country, as the need arose. I was to be of service in dealing with any language problems they might have. In addition, I was to assist them socially and academically. I saw my function more as being available to them than as initiating inquiries regarding their needs. Perhaps if they, particularly the girls, had not sought me out as much as they did, I would have found myself playing a more active role.

But there was something about my position which made me very wanted, indeed perpetually pursued by attractive, intellectual young women, who, if one can judge from the relative dearth of male students knocking at my door, must have feigned a good portion of their supposed need for my guidance. Thus the time available for me to prepare my Master's thesis seemed chronically insufficient, and only the scantiest amount of time did I spend in contemplating my future, being far too involved with my present. Everything about this job made me feel good about myself.

As I launched into my work, everything else seemed to fall by the wayside, including, maybe predictably, my ties with Ruth. Our parting was not exactly abrupt and not exactly gradual. She understood that my new job required me to move into the dorm at Mt. Scopus, but she was unprepared for the changes that took place in me as a result of the circumstances of the summer. From Ruth's point of view, as I would surmise later, we had given ourselves, body and soul, to each other and had a bond that should have lasted longer than it did, or at least should have ended in a different manner, for a different reason. In some of my more spiritual thinking at a much later time I would mystically come to see my suffering as some kind of divine retribution for my behavior toward Ruth.

In a manner of speaking I was more of an innocent than she. I had too many girls and didn't know what to do with them. When Ruth entered the world of sexual experience, her eyes were wide open, and her reasoning powers were functioning properly despite initial reticence. By the time we began to engage in sexual relations we already had established a strong bond of intimacy and trust. Although our relationship ended badly, it can not reasonably be said that her decision to be sexually intimate was ill-advised. However, the sexual decisions which I was to make during the '79-'80 academic year were those of utter innocence, unpreparedness, and lack of foresight.

2   *A Pair of Blue Eyes*

One cool, humid evening in early summer I took a walking tour near the dorms. The wind was blowing as always. The sound of crickets was all around me. It was a feeling of restlessness that had sent me on this walk in the first place, but the unusually gloomy grayness of the sky only augmented my awareness of my discontent.

Suddenly I became conscious of the sound of crying and turned to see three American girls standing off to one side. Two were attempting to comfort the third, the tallest, whose sobbing did not seem about to lessen. I approached, introduced myself, and offered to be of assistance, emphasizing that aid of this sort might well fall within the range of my responsibilities as a counselor. However, the two helpers rejected my offers and urged me to move on. I might have given up more readily, but I really felt the need to do something. It seemed to me they thought I was trying to make a pass at one or maybe all of them.

Although I was genuine in my desire to help, I did not fail to notice the large blue eyes behind the tears, and the pretty face that accompanied them. The young woman almost seemed to be smiling at me through those tears. It occurred to me that she might be suffering from a bad case of homesickness. Suddenly finding oneself in an unfamiliar environment far from home can be a most unsettling experience for some students. I tried to reassure her that things would work out happily during the year and that she would grow to feel at home.

Before leaving the group, I let her know where she could contact me if she needed help. Her name was Laura.

In August, some weeks later, I attended a lively party in the dorms. Amidst the singing and dancing I spotted a pair of familiar blue eyes. I recognized Laura almost immediately and noted that she sat conversing with Elaine, a girl I knew casually as being rough and rather abrasively direct. As Laura spoke to her, I had the distinct impression that she was asking Elaine about me.

Moments later, true to form, Elaine was upon me.

"Do you like that girl?" she inquired, pointing out Laura.

I felt embarrassed and stammered something like "Yes, maybe."

She went on to tell me that Laura was seeing a Zvi, a journalist, but would not look unfavorably upon taking me on as well.

I really did have some interest in Laura, but didn't feel quite comfortable in approaching her that evening, and nothing further happened between us then.

During the remainder of the party I had a number of tempting offers. Being sought after all the time does wonders for the ego, but, for me, it seemed to have the effect of leaving me with little opportunity to direct my life and to develop a modicum of expertise in making sound choices in my own interest.

I wound up leaving the party with Shelly, a girl I'd met several months earlier through my friend Michael.

I thought about Laura from time to time, but didn't get around to approaching her.

Two weeks later the university organized a trip to the Sinai Desert. It was to be a special project to guide American students through that wilderness so that they might gain an appreciation of its natural wonders and historical significance. The trip, in addition, was to affect the unification of the students through their sharing in a series of sublimely memorable experiences.

Hour after hour our buses rolled along, passing through vast stretches of hot, yellow, dusty, treacherous land.

It was my self-declared mission as leader of one of the busloads to see that "my" students did not miss any of the impact. I wanted them to experience the awesome beauty of the desert as I had always known it. I wished them to see how the people of Israel left Egypt and lived in Sinai for forty years until reaching the Promised Land. I wanted them to know the exotic world of the Red Sea and to live through the adventure of traveling for miles in a wadi before reaching an oasis. All this I yearned to share with them.

And share it with them I did. The special charm of the desert, with all its varied faces and primeval mystery, etched itself into our souls and bonded us together.

The desert has a unique essence, one not quite belonging to any other natural setting. It can surprise and affect people in many ways. Though not a locale where most of us would wish to live, it is a place for experiencing at its profoundest. No doubt the desert's enchantment lies in its being a world unto itself, a world where the tension and competitiveness of daily life evaporate from consciousness, to be replaced by relaxation and the sensation of oneness with the earth. In the desert a person can be alone and intimate with the greatest things ever created — the sun, the moon, the stars, the wind.

Before entering, a visitor is often frightened to contemplate nature's power, mystery, and ruggedness, but, once in, he grasps, with unexpected suddenness, the true meaning of the desert. Surely the contrast between American college students and Bedouins, whose customs have changed little in twenty centuries, is enough to jolt one into the realization of how far some of us have moved away from our roots and maybe from ourselves.

The high point of our excursion was to be the ascent to Mt. Sinai. The climb is of about four hours' duration, and the way to do it, for both practical and aesthetic reasons, is to start out not long after midnight. In this way physical exertion occurs during the coolness of night, and arrival shortly precedes sunrise, a sight which, from that peak, challenges the greatest poets to describe it.

We commenced our climb at 1:00 in the morning and continued non-stop over the rough terrain, assisted by flashlights. The brisk wind and the incredibly brilliant stars provided constant companionship. At various points along the way many of the girls said they couldn't continue, but, knowing them all to be appropriately healthy for this trek, I urged them on. Indeed we all assisted each other. The sharing and the helping in this magical setting unified us as nothing else could have done.

We succeeded in arriving just before sunrise, and all sat down, exhausted, but well aware of the magnitude of our accomplishment.

Among our fellow pilgrims atop the mountain was a small group of Yemenite Jews. In custom and dress the Jews of Yemen are known to resemble more closely the Jews of centuries past than Jews emanating from anywhere else on earth today. Their presence thus delighted me because I knew that it would enable my students, most of whom were modern American Jews, to feel more keenly the Biblical history that surrounded us.

In awe we all watched the sky gradually turn radiant with the color and the glory of the rising sun.

The pageant unfolding before us nearly exceeded the capacity of my soul to experience it. The sky became a brilliant, peaceful blue, with the most vividly glorious reds painted across the wide horizon. The mountains, of frenzied, wild shapes, took on deep, burning browns, reds, and yellows.

We watched this unearthly panorama, and, accompanied by the fresh morning wind, sang "Good Morning, Sunshine." Just to recall the occasion brings back some of the majesty of what we saw and what we felt.

If, within all of this, I should have to pick out one moment that surpassed the rest, it was the instant when the first sliver of the sun itself became visible. The experience of moving from total darkness into the utter splendor of that sunrise recalled Genesis. I felt I could understand the meaning of Creation. Silent communication with the others told me that they could too. We were as close as people could be to God. Could Moses himself have felt more than we? From that point on, I could truly say I had been to the mountain.

The singing resumed. "Glory, glory, hallelujah!...," they rejoiced.

Suddenly my gaze caught Laura's. The beautiful blue eyes were smiling and singing as much as the voice. The sight of her seemed to climax all that I had just experienced. I felt passionately that, after those moments of brilliancy, there must be some continuation. Was this to be with Laura? Was some divine plan at work here? Or did our eyes meet at this wondrous moment just by chance?

We descended Mt. Sinai with greater ease and inestimably greater wonder than we'd known on the way up.

The group headed on to Santa Katharina Monastery, a stirringly unforgettable experience in its own right, and spent a good part of the day going through it.

We set up camp in the evening of this long day some fifty miles away, at Sharm el Sheikh, on the shores of the Red Sea.

We sat around singing far into the night. With high spirits and our own music echoing in our ears we bedded down under the starry, velvet-black sky.

The Red Sea is well known for its underwater grandeur. The eyes are assaulted by the splendor of an adult fairyland of brilliant colors and varied shapes in both the coral reefs and the plants, fish, and other animals. Every color on earth hurls itself at your eyes, as if in fierce competition with every other. Among the less colorful animal inhabitants are sharks.

Almost at the crack of dawn we prepared to swim in the Red Sea. I cautioned the students to stay in groups for their safety, particularly from sharks. Although the likelihood of a shark attack was remote, one could not be too safe. I also felt I had to tell them that menstruating girls ought not to enter the sea in the first place because of the sharks' incredible ability to detect even small amounts of blood in the water.

I wondered what the girls thought of me for making this sexual reference. Weird fleeting notions passed through my head. Did they think I was trying to isolate the girls who had their periods so that the "available" ones, by their presence in the water, would immediately make themselves known to me? Maybe they thought I was the only shark around. I bit on the side of my mouth to conceal my amusement at this silly improbability.

At any rate this particular warning did not seem to linger long on anyone's mind. Most students swam; a few did not; and even I did not much notice the difference.

However, it must be said that sex was hardly absent from my thoughts. I took great pleasure in peering through my goggles underwater at the bodies of the girls, whose heads cheerfully and unsuspectingly bobbed in the sun-filled air above. In my own mind I held a contest to determine the girl with the best figure. Shelly won.

Our ride back northward to Jerusalem took us largely over unpaved, bumpy roads and was about as uncomfortable as a bus ride could be — from the physical standpoint, that is.

On the way, we made a rest stop near a 1956 war monument, on which was inscribed a poem about friendship. I translated for the group.

The poet stressed the importance of learning to distinguish genuine friendship from the counterfeit variety. Having a true friend enables one to transcend joy. Friendship can be most carefully scrutinized and reliably tested in difficult situations, on the battlefields of life, so to speak.

How appropriate, I mused, in light of this group's experiences of sharing, cooperating, and enjoying each other. Friendship among these students, young people who had hardly known each other before, solidified more rapidly in the desert than it would have anywhere else.

Back in Jerusalem one could soon observe the approach of autumn. The warmth of summer slowly became just a memory, remaining only in the warmer hues of the leaves. The wind grew more intense, and, of course, the air became cooler.

During this quieter season, seemingly designed for reflection, I came down with the flu.

I had not, since Sinai, seen much of Laura, For reasons very unclear to me I had not gone after her. I had not sought out the blue eyes that sang of the glory of creation. Was I so accustomed to being pursued and to having my female companionship determined only by the females themselves that my ability to follow up my intentions had atrophied — if ever it had existed?

I think that the very question did not enter my mind until Laura started pursuing me.

My flu clearly provided her with a golden opportunity. One day she came to my room and expressed great sympathy for poor suffering me. She prepared hot tea and saw that I took my medication. She kept me company and even cleaned my room. I sensed that she wanted something.

When night came, she jumped into my bed. I was startled. I was also ill, weak, and, I assumed, very unattractive. Stalling for time I asked how on earth she could wish to make love with the wretch that I was.

"I don't care," she said. "I want you."

As quickly as possible I tried to assess the situation. My mind bounded back and forth between thoughts of Laura's assistance to me and thoughts of her desire for me.

At the time, I saw her behavior in strictly business terms; she was negotiating the exchange of my sexual services for her domestic and medical ones. In retrospect I came to regard her actions more in terms of higher human feelings. That is to say that she liked both me and my body and did her utmost, in the only way she knew how, to find favor with me both personally and sexually.

My handling of the situation was guided by compassion for her feelings and a wish to keep alive the possibility of a relationship. Just as she had used my flu as a means of getting closer to me, I now used it as a means of warding her off. I told her that I felt so miserable as to be thoroughly incapable of doing justice to any sexual encounter. I didn't say that I preferred an intimate relationship to be more spontaneous, genuine, and natural, but I did feel just so. If there was truly a chance for us to relate as a man to a woman, that relationship would have to consist of more than hot tea and physical contact.

Try as I did to spare her feelings, she became flustered and upset. I felt helpless to do more than to utter a few words of comfort and gratitude and to leave her with some hope that we could see each other again.

With all the complexities of each human personality it's a wonder that far more relationships are not beset by the haunting conflicts and mixed feelings that have characterized my own. I liked Laura. I was fascinated by her. I found her sweet and pleasant, as well as cooperative, thoughtful, and generous. Yet I couldn't help but be annoyed by her jumping into my bed. It suggested an unsupportable shallowness. I was captivated by her lovely face, the big blue eyes especially. Yet her body was too heavy for me to want to hold her tenderly. It had no curves for me to caress. I was sexually drawn to her in some strange way. Yet I could very easily do without having sex with her.

One night I attended a birthday party which happened to be held in Laura's room. We gravitated inevitably toward each other, and, when the party broke up, we took a walk outdoors.

The night air was pleasantly cool. We reached a point not far off, overlooking the Mount of Olives and a sizable chunk of Jerusalem. As ever, the wind was blowing, and the sight of the city below put me in the mood for romance.

We drew close to each other. I started to kiss her. The soft, sensuous flesh of those lips I found incredibly sweet. Her lovemaking communicated to me an appealing shyness, accompanied, oddly, by some quality which convinced me that she was experienced. My hands passed over her breasts, which pleased me as much as her lips. I continued for some time, deriving immense pleasure from kissing her lips and fondling her breasts. I judged that she, too, enjoyed the experience, despite her laughter, as if tickled, when I first put my hand into her blouse.

At some point during this episode the thought came to me that Laura would some day be my wife.

When we returned to the dorms, I sensed that she wanted to come to my room although she didn't actually say so. I couldn't explain to myself exactly why I didn't want her there. Despite the pleasure I'd derived from her body only minutes before, I did not feel toward her a desire sufficient to drive me onward.

On the following night she came to my room. Impulsively I decided to engage in sex with her. It was worth trying, I figured. No, I didn't really figure. I just acted.

The preliminaries lasted only a few minutes and were wholly unromantic. We removed our clothes. She opened her purse and took out a diaphragm, which she started to insert in front of me. I was very surprised by what she was doing and nearly as surprised by how upset I was becoming in watching this performance. I felt that she had no respect or tact, and I hastily told her so. I found this act a most unaesthetic one for a woman to perform in front of a man, something too intimate even for people who are about to be lovers.

Laura became utterly confused. I knew that I could not have hurt her more deeply. The only thing I could do was to turn aside and let her finish privately with the diaphragm. A few quiet moments passed. Then I heard her crying. I turned to her and asked her to come close to me. I kissed her and held her gently, trying to relax her. A portion of my sensibilities continued to smart from what she had just done, which I still regarded as contemptible, yet I felt a protectiveness and closeness to her that enabled me to go on. We engaged in a satisfactory sex act, and I discovered myself dozing off on her body.

In the morning we awoke to a gently steady rainfall. Laura wished to stay in the room to do some studying. I had to leave, but I allowed her to remain and even gave her a key. Strangely she assumed that the receipt of the key gave her free access from then on. I had intended her to keep it only for the remainder of the day or for a few more days at the most. I assumed that she understood my intention. Right now I'm not sure whose assumption was stranger. The truth is that she did return the key at one point, and I held on to it for about twenty-four hours. Then she managed to coax it away from me again and did not give it back.

I grew accustomed to her frequent visits and sleep-overs in my room. I became increasingly accepting of her presence, but never really came to enjoy it. Each day, when I returned to the room, it was filled with smoke, because of which I once jokingly threatened to break up with her. She became angry, and I dropped the subject. On the day when I returned my key to her she became a permanent resident.

One noteworthy disadvantage to being Laura's boyfriend, or whatever I was to her, was that, for ethical reasons stemming from the position I held, I could not often be seen with her.

A few weeks after moving in, she announced that she'd wished to make a party for her upcoming birthday. I agreed and decided to give her a gift of a pair of candle holders for the Sabbath. A small private party, I reasoned, would not provide a vehicle for a public airing of our relationship.

The party, it turned out, served as an instrument by which I learned a great deal about Laura, which had never before come to my attention. For one thing she seemed happier than I had ever seen her. I could not have imagined a small child displaying greater exhilaration than she in opening her presents. She showed particular happiness upon unwrapping my candle holders and declared that she would light candles every Friday night. One of her friends had made a delicious carrot cake for the occasion, and Laura was full of gratitude.

She remarked to me that this birthday was far better than last year's. My own impression, gleaned from all I was observing, was that the ongoing fête was probably better than all the previous ones as well. I could see that Laura loved people, but seemed to need friends rather than to have them. The friends, or, I should say, guests, did not seem to admire her. They came, I suspected, not because they cared for Laura, but because parties are fun. My image of Laura was suddenly that of someone utterly lacking self-confidence. Whether that lack was the cause or was the result of her deficit of friends, I could not then even guess. Whenever I looked at the photographs which I snapped on that occasion, I saw a blue-eyed face beaming with happiness, which perhaps only I knew did not extend very far behind the lovely façade.

Not long afterwards I led a group of students on a trip to the Galilee and the Golan Heights. On this excursion I felt keenly the need to keep our relationship under wraps. Laura was hurt when I reminded her of this need, but accepted my decision.

In Tiberias I was sitting with some people in an outdoor cafe by the Sea of Galilee. Seeing Laura look at us from a distance, I sensed that she wanted to join us. I called her over and offered to buy her tea or coffee. Although I had to refrain from embracing or kissing her in front of the others, I certainly did not have to avoid her completely, and I enjoyed making her happy.

This trip, uneventful in most respects, enabled me to learn, by observing and analyzing, that Laura was sure I cared deeply for her.

Actually, at this stage in our relationship, my positive feelings for her outweighed my negative ones. I thought of Laura's appearance more in terms of her sweet face than of her inelegant body. I even invited her to my parents' house for dinner one Friday evening. She also became acquainted with my older sister, Gilda, who was then living in Jerusalem with her husband and two young sons. Laura felt free to visit her and my parents whenever she liked.

Clearly Laura and I had grown very attached. In a way, I could honestly say I loved her, but, at the same time, I was sure I disliked her. I still saw a few other girls, but thought of her as special. In talking with her, I made no secret of my ambivalent feelings toward her. I thus felt satisfyingly free to express with her a whole range of emotions — anger, tenderness, sadness, joy, and others. I doubted that she allowed herself the same freedom and even that she was capable of experiencing life intensely enough to need it. The relative freedom that I took for myself gave me the feeling that I dominated her. I had the odd sensation that in so doing I could feel more vigorously like a man.

This, then, was the state of affairs between me and Laura as of the winter of 1980. She satisfied some of my needs, but gave me no great highs. I did not look forward to being with her. My heart skipped no beats at the sight of her approaching. I couldn't talk with her about anything very deep; I didn't even try. Yes, I had grown attached to her, but the attachment was stifling. It was easier for me to maintain the *status quo* than to make what would have been for me a monumental decision. There would have been a big scene. I would have hurt Laura's feelings. I would have had all kinds of doubts and fears about giving up the closeness, the familiarity, the blue eyes...

3   *Barbara of the Bushes*

One day in March I was walking through the park on the Givat Ram Campus. Not far away, headed in the opposite direction, was a striking blond girl, who caught my attention immediately, and of whom I took note in more than a casual way.

On the following day I saw her on campus again. For the moment I became keenly aware of the fit of her jeans and the fall of her hair on the green jacket she wore. Something about her appearance made my heart race. I thought she might have noticed me too, but we continued on in different directions.

Several days later our paths crossed for the third time. Standing on line in the campus cafeteria I chanced to turn around and discovered her on line just in back of me. The adrenaline started flowing again. I carried my coffee and cake to the cashier, paid, and sat down at a table. Within a minute she was seated at an adjacent table, as alone as I. Somehow we began a conversation, and she got up to join me at my table.

Almost immediately we could feel the chemistry, like some invisible, agitated entity, constantly hovering over the air space between us. I could see that her face had grown red and knew myself to be blushing as well. I learned that her name was Barbara.

I embarked upon what must have been a brief discourse about myself — my family, my job, my ambitions, my present place of residence, and a host of other bits of information, opinions, and feelings that people who are trying to become acquainted can be counted on to tell each other.

Barbara, for her part, had as much as I to relate. She came from Illinois and was now living in the Rehavia section of town with a boyfriend and working for her Master's degree in Arabic. Her father was a lawyer, and her mother, a physician. Her older brother was studying law at N.Y.U. As it turned out, I knew Barbara's sister and older brother from an Israeli summer camp we'd been in together in 1970. This brother had gone out for some time with a girl I'd also dated. How small the world was, I thought.

Before we took leave of each other that afternoon, she gave me her number, and we arranged to meet on the following night. Because of her boyfriend, not to mention Laura, we decided on a neutral place, the Plaza Hotel, as our meeting point.

At about ten o'clock the next night we met there and greeted each other almost bashfully. I was pleased to be in a section of town where it seemed unlikely I'd encounter anyone I knew from the dorm. A host of unpleasant feelings came to me as I conjured up images of how Laura — and others as well — might react upon learning of this rendezvous. Indeed I was determined to maintain secrecy in both directions. At this point I hadn't any way of gauging how Barbara might react if she were to learn of my relationship with Laura.

We decided to walk to a nearby hotel with a piano bar. It was a cozy, darkened place with quiet, relaxing music, which should have been conducive to comfortable conversation. Nevertheless we didn't speak very much; I said even less than she. It was not that there was any bad feeling between us; rather, we seemed to be communicating on a different level. We gazed into each other's eyes. I sensed that I was transparently divulging my desire for her and that she longed for me too.

I wondered whether my eyes didn't also betray the uncertainty I felt about this new friendship, or whatever it could be called at that point. I myself didn't know why I felt this way, since I was hardly a neophyte in the business of relating to new women.

We left the piano bar shortly before midnight. The spring night was delightfully breezy, and the clear, fresh Jerusalem air carried the aroma of flowers. We walked alongside the walls of the Old City, speaking occasionally, mostly just looking at each other. When we arrived at the Armenian Quarter, the church bell rang, indicating midnight. At practically the same instant we heard the muezzin's cry from the minaret nearby.

It was a very special moment — tailor made for dreamers and lovers. We put our arms around each other and kissed — tentatively at first, and then with greater abandon. Her body felt soft and curvy, and her face was like silk. Feelings of passion welled up in me, but to relinquish control over my desires would have forced me to act counter to the spirit of the moment. That nagging uncertainty subsided for a while.

It was probably a few minutes before we continued on. We headed for the Western Wall. As it came into view, we slowed our already leisurely pace, finally halting altogether, and stood at a distance of a few hundred feet, studying that awesome structure. Despite the hour a number of Orthodox Jews were still praying there.

The sight of the Wall, the people praying at it, and the soldiers guarding it stimulated us to conversation of considerably greater substance than we'd had all evening. We discussed whether there was a God. We delved into the meaning of life and surged impetuously onward to solve all of humanity's problems in the space of an hour. I recall being slightly surprised by the intensity of Barbara's feelings about the Wall. If I had had any doubts before about the keenness of her mind, I surely had none now. This is not to say that I would not shortly come to question her stability, good judgment, and common sense.

We continued walking and were now in the Jewish Quarter of the New City. It occurred to me that there was nothing either sad or jovial about Barbara. Although she seemed to be into everything in life, I found it difficult to imagine her either laughing or crying. She appeared as attracted to me as I was to her, yet seemed so blasée in relating to me that I could feel neither entirely comfortable nor altogether dazzled.

The two of us moved on through the Jewish Quarter. We saw many Yeshiva boys studying by lamp light as they sat at their windows. We passed a place which I knew to have been at one time an infirmary for lepers. We discussed the fact that leprosy had actually existed in Israel. What must it be like, we wondered, to have such a loathsome disease as to be scrupulously avoided by everyone without it? We agreed that it was too depressing and, at any rate, too inconceivably removed from any experiences we'd ever had, to be worthy of further attention by us. It was growing late, and we decided to head for Barbara's apartment.

We stood on the pavement in front, conversing lightly, kissing a little, smiling at each other. Again I began to have a strange, uncomfortable feeling about her. Although she asked me up, I chose not to go. We kissed good night and agreed to get together the next day.

I returned to the dorm and spent the night with Laura.

The next evening Barbara and I met in the campus library. We sat off to one side talking for over an hour. More and more she seemed to be opening up new worlds to me. In her was a receptivity, an understanding, a confirmation. I could speak to her and get some feedback. My thoughts did not simply leave my lips and continue on out to infinity like the screamings of a person alone in the desert. I believe I provided the same type of response for her thoughts. The chemistry between us was growing. It was no wonder I kept ignoring those uneasy feelings.

Up to this point we'd done nothing more than the most rudimental hugging and kissing. For all the lack of advanced sex, I didn't happen to think myself terribly deprived because I always regarded sex punctuated with communication as keenly pleasurable even while it stayed in the beginning stages.

Barbara suggested we go outside for a while to enjoy the fresh air. On campus, a very short distance from the library, we found a secluded spot, surrounded by bushes. Once again she and I were enveloped by the fragrance of a spring evening in Jerusalem. And once again I embraced her and caressed that lovely porcelain face. From my point of view it was all a pleasantly romantic experience. Apparently it was not exactly the same for Barbara. I kissed her lips gently again and again.

Rather suddenly — and completely unexpectedly for me — she removed her jeans. It took me about one second to size up the situation: It was dark; we were completely hidden by the bushes; there seemed extremely few people in the vicinity, and none really close to us.

Despite my expectation of a far less intense encounter, I was sufficiently aroused to respond with minimum delay. Although I really liked Barbara, my romantic mood was broken. The act was very pleasurable; it simply lacked the communication and the tenderness that I thought it would have had under more conventional circumstances. My suspicion to that effect would, before long, be put to the test.

Almost immediately afterwards that same uneasy feeling returned. I could never explain it to myself, but, for some reason, I decided to take a break from Barbara for a few days. I spent time with other girls — girls from the dorm. Still I kept thinking about Barbara. I felt I should attempt to shake myself free of wanting her, but I wasn't really trying. I knew I'd seek her out again. With Barbara my senses were alive; I had a sharper, clearer taste of life's possibilities than with anyone else. She wasted no time, as I surely had seen from her performance in the bushes. But it wasn't that alone. She crammed in more living than I could have imagined possible. I found that being a part of her life enabled me, in some small measure, to do the same.

Before she left for America to visit her family, we had several more dates, each terminating in lovemaking at her apartment.

With Barbara, making love sent me to new heights. The initial stages were always cozy, yet exciting. The feel of her shapely, satiny body in motion against mine nearly drove me mad, and the rest of the world ceased to exist during those times. These exquisite feelings mounted to the point of incredible sensual ecstasy, and she took me to a higher climax than I'd ever known.

Each time, however, I could feel myself falling very rapidly back to earth as that old uneasy feeling took over my spirit. But there was plenty to keep me coming back for more. Here was the other side of my life — the flip side of Laura.

I needed a change from Laura because of dissatisfaction on a number of counts. I allowed her to remain in my room for two reasons: First, having simply grown accustomed to the arrangement, I found it easier to let her stay than to deal with the question of how I really felt about her; and, second, like Barbara, she was soon to leave Israel anyway.

Laura expected me to behave like a father to her. She would cry every night with one sort of complaint or another about how life was treating her. It's not that I was too selfish or preoccupied to lend a sympathetic ear to a friend, especially one who was sharing my room. It's simply that the tears and the chronic bad mood just wore me down. I felt myself to be carrying far more than my share in the shoulder-lending department. I wanted a relationship of equals. I had a few concerns of my own, which, under other circumstances, I surely would have shared with Laura, but there just never seemed the possibility of any interest on her part, let alone feedback. Her chain smoking didn't help matters either. She reminded me of a locomotive. My telling her so paved the way for much disagreement, which only added to the already self-destructive character of our affiliation.

As if Laura needed any more negative attributes, I came to care less and less for her sexually. I thought of her as being a few sizes too big for my body. Her figure was not slim or graceful. I didn't long for it or dream about it; I merely accepted it as one accepts a massive, heavy overcoat. It's uncomfortable and unpleasant, but it serves a purpose. Not that the same purpose could not have been served by others, most notably Barbara, but it's a great deal easier to shed something inanimate than to separate oneself from a lover who is both manipulative and temperamental, and who, in addition, has become as comfortable as an old pillow.

For her part, Barbara was preparing to leave for America for a short visit to her family. We decided to spend together the last day before her departure. I met her across town since we didn't wish to be seen by any people either of us knew.

It was a beautiful, sunny day, and we decided, on the spot, to hitchhike to the Jerusalem Forest.

Alighting nearby, we looked at Theodor Herzl's tomb and walked slowly, hand in hand, through the military cemetery surrounding it, passing hundreds of soldiers' graves. This was the price, we concluded, for living in Israel.

The young men interred there were my contemporaries, but, while they knew the sleep of eternity, I was walking in the sunlight with a beautiful girl. The guilt I felt just to have survived the Yom Kippur War myself prevented me from expressing myself sexually, even in the gentlest way, in their presence.

All the flowers around us were in full spring bloom. It was noon. We passed by the graves of Israel's leaders and arrived at the forest. Our walking turned to hiking as we made our way past the innumerable cedar trees.

After a while we sat down on a large flat rock in a clearing. There was a welcome peacefulness all around us, and everything felt just right. Nature was everywhere, to be relished by all the senses. The birds were chirping. The air was fragrant. The softness of Barbara seemed to fit in perfectly with all else that surrounded me. She removed her blouse, and I lost myself in that splendid, delicate softness. I would surely miss Barbara while she was away.

Suddenly there came an unexpected, brief rustling from the bushes. We were not alone. It took me but a second to identify the unmistakable black suit and hat, and I quickly turned back so as not to embarrass the Yeshiva boy who was peering at us through the bushes, no doubt anticipating an eyeful of passionate sexual activity. Both amused and concerned for this young man's dignity, I took Barbara in my arms, kissed her, and whispered to her of my discovery in the bushes. She decided it would be fun to give him a show, even to excite him. I went along with the idea.

It was amazing how many suggestions I had gone along with in the past year or so. I couldn't come up with much in the way of direction for my life. I was drifting rather pleasantly, and, as long as a proposal wasn't malicious, I usually yielded.

We continued kissing and caressing, but the peace of the day was broken into by the presence of the intruder, not to mention my vague inclination to burst out laughing at the ridiculousness of this scenario.

I began to feel quite uncomfortable about what we were doing, unaccustomed as I was to staging performances of this sort. I whispered that we should bring this show to a close. Barbara agreed, and, with a gesture of feigned carelessness, threw a small stone off in the boy's direction. Having tremendous compassion for the sensibilities of others, I struggled to keep from laughing. We changed our location to a point some twenty feet away. I nearly lost my struggle when I observed that he was actually moving through the bushes in pursuit of us!

That was it. Barbara put on her blouse, and we left. I accompanied her back home.

Oddly we took a rather uneventful leave of each other. I knew I'd be seeing her after her return from America. Meanwhile I needed a respite from her. I had to think through all kinds of feelings. Despite my yearning for the passion I knew with Barbara — maybe because of it — I was sure that my life needed some punctuation marks. Since Laura was about to depart for Switzerland to visit friends, I was in a situation of having two significant relationships, entirely independent of each other, come to a screeching halt, albeit temporarily.

After arriving back at the dorm from my date with Barbara, I encountered Laura and endured more sad tales and more tears. I remember feeling a faint shiver of exhilaration in anticipating her going off to Switzerland.

For the next three weeks I resolved to keep pretty much to myself. It seemed to me that I was getting a badly needed rest from both Barbara and Laura. I decided to sit back and to let happen whatever destiny had in store for me.

In so doing I became acquainted with Nadine, one of the girls from the dorm. I saw myself as being in the same situation as when I'd started on this job; once again my position as counselor provided me with the exposure and the prestige that drew the girls to me. I liked Nadine very much. She was a lively, pleasant person. I admired her beautiful singing and guitar playing. Yet a certain feeling of being a rubber stamp hung over me. I was seldom really deciding what to do, whom to befriend, or when, where, and how to love.

At any rate, when Nadine found out about my involvement with "other girls", as she put it, she was hurt and somewhat abruptly discontinued our relationship. Although I hadn't been acquainted with her long enough to experience a profound sense of loss, I had a lingering, uneasy feeling that perhaps there was more of a loss than I realized. I felt I was being taken over by forces I couldn't control or understand.

At the beginning of summer Barbara returned from America. For some reason I preferred to keep my distance. A person who is in charge of his life doesn't hold such a preference merely "for some reason". He has clear, specific grounds, even if they're as simple as disliking her or finding her uninteresting. I do recall feeling uncomfortable thinking about her boyfriend in Jerusalem and being quite nearly certain that she had recently seen another, or maybe several others, in Illinois. But a girl's having other boyfriends had never before made me avoid her. If anything, it had made the girl in question appear more desirable. With Barbara it was different.

My first encounter with her after this break occurred in the library. Working diligently on my thesis, I happened to raise my head and saw Barbara sitting a few tables away. She apparently had spotted me a bit earlier. Wearing what immediately struck me as an extraordinarily sexy dress, she was smiling from ear to ear and appeared very excited and glad to see me. Although I preferred, even at that moment, that our reunion should be low key, still I knew I was returning much the same delighted expression as she; my heart was pounding with excitement, and desire filled my body to the point where I seemed no longer to be thinking, only feeling.

We left the reading room and found an isolated corner in a remote part of the building. The anticipation, as we sought this spot, was so sweetly unbearable as to be nearly an end in itself, but holding her yielding body close against mine and savoring the incredibly soft skin of her face and the tenderness of her lips as I kissed her were more than I could take without bursting, or so it seemed.

Returning to our senses somewhat, we strolled out of the building and off campus. We walked at a leisurely pace in the direction of her apartment. The sun was beginning to set, and I would soon be unburdened of the throbbing in my body.

Meanwhile we talked. Barbara told me how elated she'd been by the visit with her family. She was imbued with the whole concept of family and considered herself eminently fortunate to have one like hers. We went on for some time discussing the meaning of having loved ones around us.

When we reached her apartment, the evening had turned into night, and I was prepared to indulge my senses to the fullest. I intended to abandon myself to every sweet pleasure I could wring out of the whole starry universe. If I didn't know myself as well as I have since come to, I would think it incredible that someone with these thoughts on his mind could have been determined, only a few short hours earlier, to behave casually about this meeting.

The sex act that we performed that night was among the best I'd ever experienced with anyone. Our bodies are capable of bringing us so much pleasure and so much misery. The ultimate joy, I suspect, is in the mind, but it's delivered there by the body. Does the body create its own pleasure? Does the pleasure come from the sex partner? Or does it emanate from the cosmos itself? For me that night it was as if powers from every corner of the universe visited every nerve in my body. Nothing else existed in those magic moments of climax — not my thesis, not my job, not my family, my future, or even the terrifying feeling that on this occasion, more than on any other with Barbara, I was not safe. I knew something unspoken was bothering her, but I would have felt uncomfortable asking her about it.

This sexual encounter was probably my most memorable, and it's good that it was, because its memory would have to last for a long time; it was to be the greater part of a year before I was again to engage in sexual relations with any woman.

4 *Farewell to Freedom*

It was early in the morning. Dawn was breaking. Having left while Barbara was still asleep, I was the only passenger on the bus that took me across Jerusalem to a point near the dorm. I showered and prepared for another day of academia.

Late that afternoon, determined to compensate for my decidedly inadequate rest of the previous night, I retired early and enjoyed a long, delicious sleep.

The following night, however, did not allow me the same. Rest was not to be.

I awoke in the wee hours of the morning feeling bad and itching. The feverishness and body aches I experienced were, at least, familiar to anyone who has ever been sick. It was that itching which most distressed me although I did not acknowledge my malaise to myself. I didn't understand what was happening to me. My attempting to ignore the itching didn't help; I was unable to sleep for the remainder of the night.

The next day I went about my business, still experiencing a certain amount of itching and aching, but daytime activity characteristically manages to conceal fears and sensations which the stillness of night only augments.

During my second sleepless night I discovered blisters and lesions, the presence of which could no longer allow me to delude myself into thinking that basically nothing was wrong. I understood one thing — that I was sexually contaminated.

This night was one of the longest in my life. If I had been floating in heaven two nights earlier, I was now surely plodding through hell. I was alone, not merely in that no one else was in my room, perhaps to comfort me, but in that suffering provides an eternal reminder of the egocentric predicament, forever a part of the human condition. No one can ever be another person. Despite the intimacy intrinsic to the most poignant of sexual relationships, orgasm is achieved, experienced, and sustained in total aloneness. My hellish feelings of that night, which I guessed must have been the antithesis of orgasm, I endured in similar solitude. Perhaps my pleasure with Barbara had, in a manner of speaking, made the gods jealous. Had the bill finally come due? Whatever might be the philosophical explanation for this nightmare, if there was indeed a cause beyond the purely physical, I was alone, I was suffering, and the sun, it seemed, would take forever to rise.

When, finally, early morning came, I did what had to be done. I went to a skin doctor. After examining me, he said I had scabies, a contagious skin disease caused by mites. He prescribed an ointment, which I applied for the next two days, but which served only to intensify the itching. Hence it was clear that the skin doctor had made an incorrect diagnosis.

I then consulted a second physician, this one a recent immigrant from Russia. It appeared that she knew her medicine, but her way of putting things left something to be desired. Her exact words, translated from the Hebrew, were, "It's nothing; it's only herpes."

This inane pronouncement had the effect of cutting my life in two — precisely at that point in time. There was the "before herpes," and then there was the "after herpes," the "undiscovered country from whose bourn no traveler returns," as Hamlet put it. Although I didn't yet know just what herpes was, I guess I saw in it a distinct parallel with death, as contemplated by Hamlet.

At any rate, this doctor gave me some blue ointment, which I began to apply right after my visit.

It was three or four days later before Barbara's and my paths crossed again. In the interim I continued to feel feverish and generally rotten. She acted very cool. I don't know just what prompted her to do so, but she told me that she had an infection. "Yes, I know," I replied curtly and sardonically. She didn't seem terribly surprised, and there wasn't a tremendous amount either of us had to say on the subject. Talking could change nothing. Just as a vibrant chemistry had once filled the space between us, that space was now saturated with my bitterness and her guilt. At least, after all she had meant to me, I had to give her credit for being able to feel guilt.

She must have known she had something. I recalled the inkling I'd had at our last encounter that something was disturbing her. Within my own mind I tried to defend her. Maybe she didn't know it was contagious. Maybe she got so carried away that she lost all common sense. Rubbish! Was I not now in the same position? I still experienced sexual longings, but the thought of communicating this disease to any woman whatsoever was to me so horrible that I would not even have considered any alternative but for my sense of decency to keep my sex drive thoroughly in check.

Israeli Independence Day was approaching. There was a certain holiday feeling in the air, a feeling which I was unable to experience in the usual way. I received a telegram from Laura, asking me to meet her at the airport. Holiday preparations, airport reunions, and the like — all these floated around dizzyingly in my head. The more I thought about such things, the more isolated and depressed I felt. I had to keep my secret, and I knew I couldn't very well avoid arousing some sort of suspicion if I were to shun all forms of socializing. But my inclination to stay in the room was too great for me to fight successfully. I had been spending an inordinate amount of time there. Always, it seemed, there were visitors, most of them unwelcome. Even under normal circumstances it had been difficult for me to ask people to leave. Now, being preoccupied with my secret problem, I found it utterly impossible to rid my room of the students who dropped in from time to time. Naturally I wished them to think that I was simply under the weather. I suppose they couldn't have known the truth.

Of course I did not meet Laura at the airport, and she had no idea why not. At the time of her arrival in my room, Rachel, one of the students, was visiting. I was very fond of Rachel, but I knew that there was no chance to develop a relationship. The instant Laura entered the room, Rachel got up and left. Her hasty, unexpected departure alarmed me somehow. Perhaps Rachel and Laura represented, respectively, what interested me and what was being forced on me, and my alarm was due to my witnessing the latter triumph over the former. Did I exert no measure of control over the happenings in my own life?

Laura looked elated to be back. Apparently she had decided to put off her inquiry about my absence from the airport. She was holding a big box — a gift for me, she said. I tried to look eager as I opened my present, but eagerness does not thrive in gloom. When my unwrapping revealed a high-quality stereo set, I attempted to appear grateful and happy. How truly happy I would have been if only the unthinkable had not occurred. How the heavens mock us when they force us to feign feelings diametrically opposite to those we actually have.

What should I do next? I thought frantically. I was trapped. The noose tightened as Laura began kissing me and making other unmistakable overtures. If she imagined that she was about to make up in one fell swoop for three weeks of abstinence from making love with me, she was in for a very rude shock. She certainly did not seem to be picking up any of the clues which I was convinced were emanating from my actions and appearance. I looked at her and felt my stomach sink. My heart was pounding, not from desire, but from a sense of terror. I was sure I could not tell her. Yet, moments later, the story, every last detail, came out.

In the brief stillness that ensued I could see the pain on Laura's face.

I was accustomed to her tears, but on this occasion there was an anguish behind them which I'd never before observed. I found some pitifully inadequate words to say that I would understand if she wanted to leave me and that, of course, she could take the stereo. This suggestion, it appeared, was more than she could bear. She broke down, and, although she could hardly speak, vowed to stay with me and to be of whatever help she could. I realized that, a moment before, I had experienced a split second of elation at the prospect of Laura leaving me. There had flashed through my mind some kind of gratefulness to the heavens for giving me herpes so that I could now be rid of her. Obviously my elation was short lived. Right about then the itching started up. Once again the powers of the universe were mocking my poor suffering soul — this time with the ironic juxtaposition of Laura's crying and my itching. If Dante had chosen to write into his *Inferno* a punishment for sexual excesses, or whatever I was being punished for, surely this would have been it.

Some time within the next few days Laura phoned my sister Gilda. From Laura Gilda first learned of my situation, which, curiously, I had not confided in anyone but Barbara, Laura, and certain members of the medical profession, each one for a clear, specific reason. I had not actually told anyone, as one might confide in a close friend for moral support or advice, but now, it seemed, I would have to deal with the leakage of my secret.

Gilda was concerned and confused. She decided not to contact me directly, but instead called my mother. My mother consulted my father. It's hard to say how distorted the details may have become by the time this news reached him. At any rate, my parents decided that my mother would travel to Jerusalem to visit me so as to learn first hand what was happening. I could never have guessed just how "first hand" she wanted her learning to be.

She arrived at my dorm room early in the morning and found me feeling predictably low. I had not expected my mother's visit, much less the revelation that three members of my family now knew of my condition.

Much later I would find tremendous amusement in thinking back to my mother's visit, but, at the time, I was simply afloat in a sea of misery.

After listening to a rather clinical presentation of the facts of my illness and its glum prognosis, my mother announced that she wanted to see my penis. This unbelievable request descended upon me like a ton of bricks. My gloom turned to incredulity and even anger. I ridiculed my mother's unseemly suggestion. But she did not relent. "Please," she implored, "I'm your mother!" After some fifteen minutes of her persistence, I gave in. What with my doctors, my lovers, and now my mother, my penis was slowly becoming public property.

I think I wanted my mother to win that battle. I was not just a defeated man yielding to the slightest pressure. I was more like an injured child, hoping against all sound reasoning that my trusted, devoted, sacrificing mother could make everything bad go away. But, of course, this hope was dashed.

The sight of the blisters and lesions very greatly upset my mother. "How come?" she kept asking. "My children have always been so clean."

Very soon she was joined by another mourner, Laura, who entered in the midst of my mother's head shaking. For some time my room vied with the Western Wall as the mourning capital of Jerusalem. Although I was certainly no happier than they over my situation, I regarded their carrying on as nonsense. It was difficult to be sympathetic to people whose suffering was caused by my greater suffering. Even genuine empathy can appear hypocritical and shallow to the primary victim, the one who, unlike them, can not turn away or forget. Who, after all, were they to expect consolation from me? They did not deserve the luxury of a gentle embrace or a reassuring word. For these they hadn't suffered enough.

I felt myself growing callous in my attitude toward others, particularly the people who displayed the greatest concern over me. Our loved ones are always the most convenient ones on whom to vent our anger. I was distressed by what I saw in myself. My main problem was growing offshoot problems, of which my unpleasant demeanor was surely one.

I showered, dressed, and ran off. Life must go on, I reasoned. I must get back into my work. I can not sit around feeling sorry for myself. Sorrow was something I felt, but I could not allow it to become an activity.

Every other week I was visiting a skin doctor at a Jerusalem hospital. He always smiled, it seemed, even while he was examining me. I would have preferred him to be more serious. Certainly his lightheartedness was not catching. He always told me to return in two weeks and never prescribed any medicine. The blisters came and went.

Often I found myself standing at the window of my room, gazing out at the carefree young students on the hunt. *Am I going to live with it forever?* I would ask myself.

Israeli Independence Day came. On me it had the special effect of serving as a stabbing reminder that I was no longer independent. I went to bed early. Hearing the music and dancing of the young people outside hurt me deeply. In my heart was such pain that I truly did not know how I could carry on.

Someone knocked at the door. I rose from bed to answer it. It was an old friend, who had in recent years become religious. We started to talk. This was what I needed badly. I didn't reveal my secret, but we delved into matters to which I needed to direct my attention. We brought up questions about the meaning of life. I listened as he gave his views on why we entered the world and how we should live it.

The music surrounding us became the focal point for him to express the ideas which most directly affected me. At first he simply suggested that I not alienate myself from the music and other festivities. Entertainment, he said, purifies the soul. I was about to dismiss this piece of advice because I saw no way to force myself and that music together. But he patiently explained. In pursuing entertainment one diffuses one's soul, thereby purifying and unburdening it. Being serious all the time can bring on illness or exacerbate what is already there. A person who has unburdened his soul can tackle his work more effectively and efficiently. The soul must concentrate itself, rather than spread itself out, in order for one to study, and diversions facilitate concentration afterwards. We must strike a balance between entertainment and work, and, at the same time, guard against excessive diffusion of the spirit, which results in loss of power.

I saw myself in what he said, in that I was not able to purify my soul of its sexual needs. I became determined to stop shunning all forms of entertainment; at least I could have *some* purification. From that point on, I believe I became more productive in my work and studies. I felt a little better, although for me there were no easy answers.

After he left, Laura came back to the room, where, since learning the news, she had decided to remain with me. We had been occupying separate beds since her return from Switzerland.

A few nights later I had a bad dream. I saw a small, devil-like creature that seemed to take on the shape of a spider in a web. It moved toward me and stung me. I awoke in a cold sweat, screaming, "Laura, wake up! I just saw the devil! He's been in this room! We must get rid of him!"

I turned on the light and immediately felt the compulsion to open the windows and door. Upon opening the door I discovered a large yellow spider on the floor just outside. I killed it and felt relief. How curious that the spider should have turned up just then, when creatures of that type were quite uncommon in the dorms.

After that Laura got into my bed, and we held each other close and kissed. She, too, was frightened. I calmed down somewhat as I found myself in the position of having to relax her. She fell asleep with her leg on my stomach so that I could hardly breathe or move. My awareness of her heavy frame increased. Whereas I took pleasure in the more delicate, graceful examples of the female form, I found Laura's massiveness increasingly disturbing. I moved to the other bed and remained until morning.

During this time Laura stuck with me and tried to be helpful. I saw very little of Barbara. One day I came upon her with her boyfriend and suddenly felt anger as the thought came to me that she might be the devil incarnate. Laura, on the other hand, seemed full of love for me. It seemed I could love myself only through her.

I recall one evening, when Laura and I were sitting with a group of students in one of the dorm rooms. Everyone was singing as one of them played the guitar. When he played the song "Honesty," Laura sang out with all her heart. Tears came to my eyes as I gazed at her face. She was truly beautiful. Her big blue eyes particularly melted me. What had I done to her? The academic year was nearly over, and with its termination would come her return to America, with memories of a hideous experience with me.

June came. Laura prepared her suitcases, and I looked back on the year. It was beautiful in many, many ways, but I had scars which I didn't think would ever heal. Just before I accompanied her to the airport, we spent our last hours together in Jerusalem. We held onto each other and cried and cried. I realized more than ever how attached I had become to her and how much I really loved her. I was filled with a deep feeling of loyalty to her for her steadfast friendship. When we said our final good-bye at the airport, I left with a feeling of profound emptiness.

During the next few days I spent a good part of the time by myself in my room. Most of my good friends had already left for the United States. And there I was, alone with my blisters and itching, trying to finish my thesis and my dissertation and to prepare for my final exams. With all that was going through my mind it was difficult to concentrate, but somehow I completed my work by devoting large segments of time to it, day and night. Throughout much of this period I listened on my radio to music from the *Voice of Peace*. I especially enjoyed John Lennon. His music had the effect of strengthening my spirit and giving me hope.

I successfully passed my exams and received my Master's degree. With the pressure of studying out of the way I was able to enjoy the feeling of accomplishment that was rightfully mine. I could look to the future with a clearer head.

The university asked me to remain on, acting as counselor to students coming in for summer courses. I accepted the job, but, as new waves of students appeared, it occurred to me that I might no longer have sufficient peace of mind to be able to help them.

Nevertheless I was soon put in charge of guiding a group of students to the Judaean Desert and Masada.

The desert is a place I know and love. I crave its ingenuousness. Few other natural settings can claim to be as unspoiled and uncommercialized. None, except the Antarctic, possesses the otherworldly quality of silence, a silence so penetrating that a visitor can hear his own heart say things which would never reach his awareness in any other place.

The American students on this trip were amazed. I derived tremendous satisfaction from seeing them react, indeed from transporting them back twenty centuries.

My satisfaction, of course, was marred by my own twentieth-century concern. I had an active case of herpes at the time, and the heat intensified the itching. Now how in hell do you scratch yourself out in the middle of the desert, with no place to turn for privacy, in the company of a busload of people? You don't. This is herpes in the desert.

My love affair with the desert was one more love affair that herpes prevented me from enjoying to the fullest, but herpes could never put a check on my pleasure with the desert as it was doing with more purely sexual joys. I say *more purely sexual* because *whatever* provides sensual pleasure for the heart and soul is itself sexual in nature and simply becomes more so when shared with someone who can appreciate it in the same way and whom one cares for sexually.

I looked down at the Dead Sea from Masada. With no life possible in it, it rested quietly. Small clouds slowly floated over it, adding to the sensation of total peace, a delicious peace of which I partook gratefully.

I looked at the acacia trees near where I stood. I saw the acacia as a tree of life, but a lonely tree. I could feel the whistle of the wind among its branches. The wind is a frequent companion in the desert. All around, one can see the lines it sculpts in the sand, which turns from a dry brown color to a burnt yellow in the heat of the sun.

On this excursion I felt my senses taking in more than usual. The ability to feel is no less precious than the ability to see or to hear. It goes beyond mere tactile perception of texture, temperature, and shape. It is the emotional absorption of the meaning and beauty in what nature has provided and what humanity has done with its creative impulses. Being deprived of the privilege of indulging my feelings whenever I pleased, I held jealously onto whatever sensual, emotional feasts my condition permitted me to experience.

At the spring of Ein Gedi I reveled in the sound of the flow of water. If water can gush continuously amidst vast stretches of aridity, which, themselves, can delight the heart, then you know that the desert will go on forever. Surely, then, there is some future for me.

Clearly the extreme conditions of the desert had not lost their ability to enable me, even me, to encounter the unexpected. I had counted only on a satisfying respite from my worldly concerns and had found, through a fresh interpretation of the familiar, the hope I needed to go on — for a while. The desert can also confuse you, but I clung to the expectation that my new comfort would strengthen me upon my return to Jerusalem.

As it happened, I soon discovered that life with herpes consisted of a series of alternating dejection and inspiration, sadness and comfort.

I had to decide how to relate to that summer's female students, who were causing history to repeat itself by their frequent visits to my room. Sometimes I looked at them and said to myself, *How can I give one of them such a terrible disease?* This wasn't really a question because the answer was a foregone conclusion. There was no way in this whole world, despite possible dire consequences to myself, that anyone would ever get herpes from me. I preferred simply to avoid these bright young women, except as my job required contact.

I recall a tall, blond, rich girl from Florida, who tried to make a pass at me. She would come to my room several times a day, attempting to tease me into bed. Always I put off her suggestions by wisecracking or changing the subject. One day I hugged her and said, "I know you're a virgin." As if taking me seriously, she expressed tremendous resentment and declared hotly that she was not. "So, what do you want now," I asked her, "to get herpes?"

I felt always on the defensive. I had to keep thinking of inoffensive, breezy, clever excuses as to why I would not have sex with one girl or another. How naive and vulnerable they all seemed to me.

As the summer of 1980 wore on, I had a three-week break from work. For obvious reasons I was filled with sexual desire.

By chance I met an attractive Israeli girl, Dodi, on the campus one day. Before we had spent much time together, she started doing her best to tempt me into bed, and succeeded in luring me there, no doubt because I had with her a perfect excuse not to indulge in sex beyond the point where she would be safe from contracting herpes. She had had an abortion only four days earlier and was still sensitive. She said she just couldn't wait, despite the soreness, and doubtless expected me to perform to completion. But I told her that complete sexual relations would probably be harmful to someone in her condition. We had a wonderful time in bed, stopping just short of genital contact. She must have thought me the most altruistic man alive!

That night, back in my own bed, I felt the bitterest frustration. Was it worth it, I wondered, to begin sexual activity knowing of the tremendous discomfort that would inevitably ensue? Would it not be better simply never to think about sex in the first place? If only my body and emotions could have cooperated with my mind.

In the middle of that night, as I lay steeped in frustration, trying to convince myself that there was some course of action to solve my problem, someone knocked. I opened the door and found two girls, one of whom was known to me from the dorms. She introduced the other girl as her friend Susannah, who was also a student at the university. Susannah, it turned out, suddenly found herself with no place to stay. I gave her permission to sleep in my spare bed, the one Laura had used, until I could make other arrangements for her. Some details of this story were unclear to me, but at that hour I wasn't about to press for further information. Thus did Susannah and I bed down for the night.

Susannah stayed in my room for about six weeks. Although I soon arranged for another room, as I'd promised, she kept coming to me. We became good friends in what one might call a semiplatonic way. She had an American boyfriend who was then living in California and was expected in Israel in several weeks.

I really liked Susannah. She was sharp, lively, charming, and funny. Her face resembled Barbra Streisand's.

I told her a great deal about myself, but not about my herpes. Our relationship often brought to my mind the words to a Hebrew song: *A man lives inside himself. Sometimes he opens the door. Mostly he keeps to himself.*

We spent several delightful nights hiking through the mountains and corners of Jerusalem. On a few occasions we just wandered from bakery to bakery, enjoying the smell of the baked flour.

With the growing closeness and the good times we were having together, it was only natural that we should have developed feelings for each other, feelings of belonging together.

There was no sex between us. As far as Susannah knew, I felt that sex for us would have constituted improper interference in her relationship with her boyfriend. Actually the existence of a boyfriend merely provided me with the same kind of explanation for abstinence as had Dodi's abortion. If not for the herpes, I gladly would have made love to Susannah.

With the approach of the boyfriend's arrival, Susannah made it quite plain that she wished to go to bed with me. As I had done with Dodi, I allowed my emotions to overrule my mind, of course in no way permitting a true sexual union, for both her sake and that of her boyfriend.

I removed her dress and looked wistfully at her delicate body. In one of the last melancholy days of August, we spent the night in bed together, but we both remained in our underwear, the presence of those garments deluding us into thinking that what we were doing wasn't genuinely sexual.

When she awoke in the morning, she felt very frustrated. I reminded her that her boyfriend was arriving in a few days.

On the morning of the day when he finally did arrive she was even more frustrated. She couldn't know how I sympathized with her, but I could be of no help.

When she left for Tel Aviv to meet him, I was alone again for the first time in weeks, with only herpes for companionship. I tried to relax and enjoy my loneliness. It was already September. Only a few days remained before I would have to vacate my room and move back into my parents' home. Maybe I should just run away somewhere, I thought. The very act of existing was burdensome to me at that time. I didn't know what to do with myself.

Somehow, despite the suffering, I always ended up moving forward according to plan. I did not run away or do anything else dramatic. Dramatic acts were only things to think about. I knew intellectually that they would not solve my problem, but imagining myself carrying one of them out constituted rebellion. And so, my rebellion over, I packed my bags and left the campus.

5 | *Fighting Back*

On the bus home from Jerusalem I read in a newspaper about some girls who were cured of a viral infection by a drug called Interferon. I considered my own case, herpes being a virus. Yes, I decided, at the first chance I would travel to the hospital where the cures had taken place.

I took that first chance on the following morning.

My level of confidence could not have been higher as I rode the bus from home to a point near the hospital and jumped out into the brilliant light of an early Israeli autumn. Something about seeing the world bathed in sunshine puts joy and hope into the heart. Certainly I needed plenty of both.

I don't know whether I ever enjoyed a walk more in my life. I fairly leaped along the streets past the citrus groves, eager anticipation filling my spirit.

Having located the office of the professor named in the article, I knocked at the door, gained admittance, introduced myself, and told my story. I gave no thought to whether I might be breaking into this man's busy schedule. I needed help, and he accepted me.

He believed that I could be cured, he said, but at a cost of at least three thousand dollars. I didn't care about the money.

As I left the hospital, I actually found myself whistling. Was I seeing the light at the end of the tunnel? I hoped that it wasn't emanating from an approaching train. Anyway, at least I had hope, almost as desirable an entity as a cure itself.

Later on in the day, however, my elation level began to drop. Three thousand dollars was a formidable figure. How on earth I would come up with it I had no idea.

During the next few days, as I sought to discover the manufacturer of Interferon, I learned that it was made from foreskins. Here lay the reason for its virtually prohibitive cost. I resolved to find as inexpensive a way as possible to obtain the drug and decided to try the Weizmann Institute in Rehovot.

Once there, I was informed that a certain gynecologist elsewhere in the country was about to start a program of administering Interferon to women with genital herpes. Before commencing the treatments, however, this gynecologist would be required by law to gain permission from Israel's Helsinki Committee, set up to pass judgment on new medicines. What it boiled down to was that, without this committee's green light, Interferon would not be administered to any herpes victims.

Another hurdle I had to clear consisted of being permitted into the gynecologist's group in the first place. He was, after all, working with women.

When I went to that hospital, I sat waiting in a line of women. I felt weird and wondered what they thought I was doing there. This was the very hospital where I had been born, and I now saw myself as a defective product being returned for repairs.

My turn finally arrived. The doctor spoke to me as a man to a man. Explaining that the experimental group had been set up for women because of the increased risk of cancer among female herpes victims, he agreed, nevertheless, to accept me. I returned home a trifle disappointed, however, because the doctor himself still had to await permission from the Helsinki Committee.

During this time of waiting my experience at home was nothing less than miserable. My parents would ask me every day, usually several times, "Do you have it?" Always they wanted to know whether I had any blisters, whether I had new blisters, whether the old ones were going away, how many there were, whether I was itching, etc., etc. I acquired the habit of always answering in the negative so as to avoid their feedback, which crushed me down into a pit of anguish.

"Please," I was warned incessantly, "please, please be careful of how you use the restroom." After all, it would be unthinkable for anyone else to catch herpes from me, least of all my young nephews, whom Gilda brought frequently to visit.

It was horrible for me, as it must have been for the rest of my family. For me, however, it had the added dimension of making me regard my parents, sisters, brother-in-law, and nephews as clean, pure, healthy people with everything to look forward to — if only I didn't contaminate them. I, on the other hand, was the potential contaminant, the leper. I knew that my parents and the others were worried and concerned about me. I knew it, but I didn't feel it. I was in a state of constant stress.

For some reason, I suddenly recalled that the professor at the first hospital had named a certain colleague who was also using Interferon.

Determined to leave no stone unturned, I paid a visit to his department. There I made the acquaintance of a woman who was doing research on herpes. Even before she'd identified herself, I could *smell* that she was involved with that disease.

She requested a sample of the fluid from one of my blisters and examined it under the microscope, discovering from what she saw that I had a particularly virulent form of the disease. This news wasn't exactly encouraging, but I was moving along. Standing still with no hope was what most distressed me.

In spite of this doctor's warm, agreeable manner, her evident relish in her work made me uncomfortable. Looking through the microscope myself certainly did not cause my eyes to light up as hers had done a moment earlier.

She gave me a drug in the form of a frozen liquid and instructed me to defrost it every three hours and apply it to my blisters. In experiments with eighteen people, she told me, the drug really did work.

To avoid the slightest deviation from her instructions, I stayed home for the next four days, carefully counting the hours, and applied the medicine faithfully every three hours — day and night.

Within a few short weeks I was able to notice a marked decrease in the frequency of the appearance of blisters. A three-week interval, as opposed to a ten-day interval, was a good sign. I was convinced I was on the right track. But I could not allow myself to be blinded by this first sign of progress.

My parents still put much pressure on me. They continued to ask me for progress reports. I soon realized that I was seeing myself as dirt on the ground. I felt I was losing my personality. I grew to have such contempt for myself that I could hardly believe my body and soul were sharing the same space. The very loathing that everyone around me seemed to be experiencing, I started to feel toward myself. Others, however, could avoid me. I could not avoid myself. Whatever my medicine was doing, it was not doing it fast enough, and the doubts and the fears and the disgust would continually stab at my consciousness. It seemed that every time I did something to try to improve my lot, the attempt boomeranged.

I used to spend hours on the beach in and near Tel Aviv. As evening approached, I would gaze out at the sun setting over the Mediterranean and think faraway thoughts. Somehow my wish to separate my soul from my body was being granted for a while each day. My deepest, truest, most intimate feelings and experiences had not the remotest association with my daily physical surroundings.

One warm October afternoon I decided to go into the water. The sea felt good. I was glad that my body could still bring me some pleasure, that not all of my pleasures had to stem from a mind, from which a body had been pushed aside.

On the following day I discovered some unusually large blisters. I understood that I could no longer enjoy the water, as I had in the past. I can not even try to describe the bitterness I felt.

In one way or another I still had the strength and determination to continue with my treatments. I suppose my condition would have been worse without them, but that consideration didn't comfort me much. I felt I had to escape.

An idea took shape in my mind. I would go to America. I would become involved right away with plans for a new venture. Perhaps America would have more in the way of treatment for me. I would be escaping and rebelling without really doing anything rash. Didn't perfectly rational, content people travel abroad every day? Gilda's family was temporarily living there because of her husband's job, and my younger sister, Adyli, was traveling all around the States. I would certainly not be hurting anyone by adding myself to their number. *Why not?* I thought. In all my twenty-eight years I had never once been outside of Israel. I had a goal. Once more I was filled with hope. Experience had taught me that it wouldn't last, but I had to keep dosing myself with it whenever I could. I preferred alternating highs and lows to one steady low.

I had made a decision. I bought an airline ticket and reserved a seat on a flight in mid-November. Besides the usual preparations that a traveler makes, I knew I would have to visit my beloved Jerusalem before leaving the country.

During all the time that I had been involved with checking out treatments and coming to terms with my family, the source of all my anguish, namely Barbara, was occupied with her own problems and activities.

Barbara used to hitchhike in Jerusalem. Hitchhiking in Israel is commonplace and is not fraught with the dangers inherent in that practice in many other places. But Barbara didn't just hitchhike in order to be transported to a destination. Barbara loved to hitchhike. Thumbing a ride enabled her to meet many new people and made her feel good to know how eager the young men of the city were to pick her up.

It was through hitchhiking that Barbara met my friend Eli. He had seen and admired her before and jumped when the opportunity to drive her somewhere came his way. The ride led to the establishment of a friendship between them.

Shortly before vacating my dorm room, I had had a chance meeting with Eli and thus learned of his new friendship. But Eli learned a great deal more than I from that meeting. Not to have told him about Barbara's herpes would have rendered me responsible for his eventually contracting the disease. I was as duty bound to warn him as I was to guard against communicating herpes to any woman I might make love to. I cautioned him to be extremely careful and asked that he regard this information with the utmost confidentiality. His silence was to extend to not informing Barbara that he was aware of her condition.

During the following week Eli and Barbara spent many hours together and grew very close. I guess the strain of keeping my confidence became too much for him, and the inevitable occurred. According to Eli, who phoned me at my home shortly afterwards and was straightforward enough to admit his frailty, Barbara was so shocked that she couldn't speak. He also mentioned that she tried to call me to vent her anger, but couldn't reach me. There was nothing more I cared to do or say on this matter.

But fate decreed that it should confront me again on the day I went to say good-bye to Jerusalem.

Naturally one of my stops was the Givat Ram campus. At the library I was about to descend the spiral staircase from the main lobby when I spotted Barbara walking up those stairs. I didn't know just how to react. Rather large numbers of people were standing or walking near us. Not surprisingly, Barbara had an expression of anger, even rage, on her face. For a few uncomfortable, tense moments we just stood looking at each other. The sight of her fury at first rendered me speechless. Then without exchanging any words, as if by prearranged signal, we walked toward the exit and left together, heading, as we'd done once an eternity before, toward the bushes.

We sat together on a bench by the shallow pool. Suddenly Barbara burst into tears. She sobbed uncontrollably, almost hysterically. I had never before seen her cry. Indeed I could hardly believe that someone as strong and confident as Barbara was even capable of crying. While her heart bled, mine turned to stone. I, the soft one, did not hold her or kiss her. I sat like a statue. What a tragedy, I thought, that this scene should take place on my last day in Jerusalem.

Eli had told me that Barbara's boyfriend was in a mental institution. She had doubtless been thinking in terms of developing new relationships, and, by revealing her herpes, I had placed a formidable obstacle in her way. Surely she felt abandoned on all sides. I did feel sorry for her, but I felt sorrier for me. I had to admit to myself that I was getting some satisfaction from what, regardless of my intentions, amounted to poetic justice. Here, after all, was an intelligent, sophisticated young woman, who had not taken any care to avoid giving me an unspeakable disease, and who, to that very day, consistently denied being the culprit. Now she had the chutzpah to try to send me on a guilt trip because of my effort to spare a friend the same fate.

Barbara's sobs turned a few heads. A friend of mine passed by, observed us both sitting there, and continued tactfully along. I noticed one of my professors pause momentarily as he gave a curious look.

As I studied Barbara, I realized I hadn't any more feelings for her. I just wanted this nightmarish scene to be over, but not in a good way. I preferred the wounds to remain open...

Two days later I sat on the beach and wrote her a letter outlining my feelings. I wished to remain inside myself, I wrote, not to open all my doors. I was not going to let her share my world. She would know neither the joy nor the suffering in it.

My parents, particularly my mother, were not at all displeased with my decision to fly to America. My mother had traveled there several times. She now contemplated going again and relished the prospect of being with Gilda, Adyli, and her grandsons. Because of my desire to remove myself from the familiar, I might have figured her to be an encumbrance, but I knew that she would not be hanging on to me. She had relatives to visit and sights to see. Moreover it made me feel good to see my mother have a change of scenery from her endless tasks of cooking, cleaning, shopping, laundering, typing for my father's law practice, and serving snacks to his many clients who visited our apartment nearly every evening.

For my part, I had to postpone my intended departure because of another herpes attack. My medicine could not have retained its required freezing temperature throughout the long flight. I wound up leaving a day after my mother.

Not only didn't I take the medicine with me, but I gave no thought to obtaining it in the United States, despite my earlier interest in exploring American medical possibilities. I behaved as if I were literally running away from my herpes, as if I expected it never to recur once I had crossed the ocean.

6 | *The Great Escape*

The next day, Friday, November 21, 1980, I left Israel. I shall never forget saying good-bye to my father at the airport. I knew that his pain in seeing me off far exceeded whatever he'd felt in taking leave of my mother. She would return home much sooner than I, and, besides, he didn't have to grieve for her as he grieved for me. My father and I, despite our attempts to mute our feelings, plainly were in great pain for each other. My throat was so tightly constricted that I could hardly talk. As I looked at him through the window of the plane, I fought back my tears. I had told him not to feel bad because I'd be back in a few months. Maybe that was the wrong thing to say. He was in failing health. My time reference probably made him all the more aware that this might be the last we would ever see of each other. Oh, how I read his heart as I watched him lean on the railing.

I remember the journey well. A group of Christian tourists was returning to America. They talked happily about their experiences in Israel. A woman from the group sat next to me and told me how much she loved my country, the land where Jesus had lived.

We flew over the Alps, covered with endless stretches of snow. Interminably, incredibly white, blazing in the sunlight, the mountains made me squint each time I stared down at them. My thoughts turned to Hanibal trying to cross all this. We flew over Italy, France, the Atlantic Ocean, all the while following the sun.

I spent a large part of my time thinking about my father. I tried to see my family, my country, and my herpes in perspective. An airplane is a highly suitable place for that purpose. How very small my country is, I pondered, and how large is the world!

After some thirteen hours the plane arrived in New York. Just before landing I looked down at the highways filled with cars that seemed to be racing in every direction. My initial impression of America was that everything was fast and impersonal.

At Kennedy Airport I claimed my luggage and took my turn with customs and immigration officials. It struck me that they were investigating me more closely than other arriving passengers. One of the officials asked whether I had any disease. I just said no.

I knew they had no reason to suspect me of having herpes or any other disease; so I wasn't worried about being exposed or deported. But I did experience a twinge of resentment at the irony of this particular attempt to guard against contamination from foreigners. My own disease had been contracted from an American woman, who'd gotten it from an American man while she was spending a college vacation break in America. In Israel, as I'd come to realize from my medical contacts, herpes was all but unknown.

Having emerged from all the questions, I was met by my uncle Jacob and my mother, who had spent the previous night at his house in northern New Jersey. There I stationed myself for the next six days, seeing a little of New York and visiting local relatives.

Thanksgiving was approaching, and we were all invited to the home of my mother's cousin Shuli in a suburb of Philadelphia. Since Jacob had taken ill, only four of us went down. My aunt Lucy drove, with her seven-year-old son, Aaron, my mother, and me as passengers.

Seeing Shuli gave me a great deal to think about. Only a few months older than I, Shuli seemed to have done infinitely more than I felt I could sensibly hope to have done myself. I knew I tended to measure accomplishment and success in terms of marriage and children. Probably I did not employ a very humane measuring stick, but it stemmed from my own experiences and values and was the only one with which I was familiar. At any rate, there was Shuli, with a husband she seemed to adore, a six-year-old son, and a three-year-old daughter, showing us pictures and telling us stories of their happy life. The chill in the air and the overcast skies served as an appropriate setting for my feelings of detachment and pessimism. The animated conversation didn't help either. No one there, except my mother, knew about my herpes, and neither of us wanted anyone among our relatives ever to know.

The four of us visitors stayed overnight. In the morning I awoke to two findings — one pleasing and the other depressing. The pleasing one was that cousin Aaron had wet his bed. In seeing Shuli deal with this occurrence, I released some of my hostility against a happy, conventional world, of which I felt I couldn't be part.

The depressing finding was that I had broken out in three new blisters.

Later in the morning a friend of mine from Philadelphia came to Shuli's to pick me up, and took me on a tour of the City of Brotherly Love. My mother, Lucy, and Aaron drove back to New Jersey without me. For my part, I took a bus back alone from Philadelphia at the end of a long tiring day.

Some of the most interesting people I met in the United States were my traveling companions on buses.

My seat mate on this Philadelphia-to-New York run turned out to be a beautiful blond psychologist. In her style of conversation she typified many American women I was to meet. She liberally sprinkled her conversation with, "Oh, how...!" Always the expression finished with an adjective like "nice", "beautiful", "great", "gorgeous", or "fantastic." I was unaccustomed to being bombarded with superlatives in discussions of everyday matters. Words tend to lose their meaning when overused. In Israel people are inclined to save the strongest words for more intense needs. Israelis, I started to think, do not hand out compliments as freely, and indeed come out with more negative criticism in situations where Americans would think themselves impolite to do so. I wasn't sure which way I preferred, although there was something not quite frank about the American manner. Mainly I just took note that there was a marked difference.

I arrived at the Port Authority bus terminal in mid-town Manhattan and decided to take a walking tour of the area before boarding a bus to Jacob's house.

On a post card bearing a colorful picture of Manhattan's profile, as photographed from the New Jersey side of the Hudson River, the famed island appears beautiful, dynamic, exciting, and sophisticated. It calls invitingly to poets, painters, and lovers. But in the area of my tour the beauty was nowhere to be found.

I was passing through a jungle, not one of lush, exotic vegetation, but a jungle seething with the impoverished, sick, drunk, drugged, and crazy. Depravity and begging flaunted themselves on all sides. I noticed a man with herpes on his face, sitting on the sidewalk, chewing on bread crusts. Feeling about as unsafe as I'd ever felt, I decided it was time to head for New Jersey.

Before November sang its swan song, we at Jacob's house were paid a visit by Gilda's family, accompanied by Adyli, who had been visiting them in their apartment in Brookline, Massachusetts. My New Jersey cousin's family joined us, and we had a gala family reunion. Privately Gilda asked about my health. Everything was hush-hush. I felt like a spy. But none of us ever questioned our policy of silence.

I had no way of knowing then that, even as we spoke, my secret already had leaked elsewhere into the family tree and that in exactly six days it would find its way to Jacob.

On Monday morning, December 1, Lucy drove me to the bus stop. As I sat through the hour-long ride from New Jersey into Manhattan, I thought about David, my childhood friend, whom I would now be seeing for the first time in five years.

David was born with a rusty spoon in his mouth. During our childhood together my family befriended him in various ways, and we became very close.

When I had last seen David, he had only five dollars in his pocket and was leaving Israel for New York. Now he was the wealthy owner of a big warehouse and several stores.

When he first saw me on that December day, he seemed delighted. In catching up with five years' worth of news, I learned and observed more about the new David. I learned that he was soon to replace his Mercedes with a chauffeur-driven limousine. I had a taste of his life-style when he treated me to dinner in an extravagantly appointed restaurant. The most revealing thing that he did was to hand me two hundred dollars, which I hesitantly accepted. In my uncertain situation I could not allow myself to fall into the pit of false pride. In past years my family had spent considerably more than that on him, although we were never rich.

He told me how important money was to him — as if I couldn't see that for myself. He had learned that friendship, love, and sex were merely commodities. All one needed was a show of money in order to have whatever one wanted. Unhappily I learned from subsequent observations of his behavior that there was a tremendous element of truth to what life had taught him. If we're surrounded by people who place a high value on material goods and those who possess them, then, by some rule or another of economics, they do indeed become valuable. Perhaps people whose friendship is for sale are not worth having as friends, but, if you never learned to relate to people in a different way, you might just prefer having some kind of friendship to being all alone. Maybe I was judging David very charitably. I chuckled as I pondered the question of which one of us was truly the benefactor of the other.

Later in the week I again traveled from Jacob's house to Manhattan and again spent a night with David. This time he suggested that I extend my stay in the States and go to work in one of his stores. He would pay me well, he said, and I could save up a lot of money. Perhaps I would even remain in America, as he had done. I said I'd give the matter some thought. I truly had no idea what on earth I wanted to do.

My mother having accompanied Gilda's family and Adyli to Massachusetts, I decided to make the trip up there myself instead of aimlessly shuttling back and forth between Jacob's and David's. Without returning to New Jersey I took a bus directly up to Gilda's.

Gilda's family of four occupied a small two-bedroom apartment. Every room seemed very tiny, even by Israeli standards. The space was further diminished by the presence of my mother, Adyli, me, and all the luggage we had.

It wasn't only the crowding that made my brief stay there unpleasant.

I keenly sensed that Gilda and her husband, Dan, feared for their sons. On a number of occasions I discovered Gilda cleaning the bathroom with alcohol. I made up my mind to leave although I would have loved to see more of the Boston area, with its delicious combination of youthful spirit and historical flavor. Being frankly unable to acclimate myself to a New England December, I decided to return when the weather got warmer.

7 *Frustration and Inspiration*

My next American stop was to be Kansas City, Missouri, in one of whose suburbs Laura lived. I had not seen her since her departure from Jerusalem six months before, although we carried on a voluminous correspondence. She missed me terribly, she wrote, and fervently hoped that I would visit her soon. I still had feelings for Laura — mixed though they were. Maybe there was yet hope for our relationship. Totally at loose ends anyway, I knew that spending time with her during her winter recess from college in Colorado would not exactly interfere with what was never a carefully planned vacation for me to begin with.

I took a bus trip of a few days from Boston to Kansas City. On board I contentedly lost myself in sharing small talk with refreshingly simple, ordinary people.

Laura's mother picked me up at the terminal. Although we had never met before, we had no trouble in identifying each other from photographs Laura had, in the past, shown each of the other.

As she drove me to her house, I noticed that she spoke very slowly, and I guessed that she had decelerated her speech so as to accommodate this foreigner, who might not otherwise understand her. I asked her to feel free to speak faster to me because my English was not all that bad. It turned out that my guess was incorrect. "That's the way I talk," she drawled.

The woman seemed rather cool to me. I judged that she recognized her own coolness and was making a special effort to compensate for it.

When we arrived, Laura was excited and thrilled to see me. Her father, a short, fat, bald man, behaved in a highly businesslike fashion. Unlike his wife, he made no attempt to conceal his coolness. He looked at me for a moment and asked me whether I ate pork. I replied in the negative and added that I didn't consume dairy and meat products together either. I became acutely aware of the difference among Jews in various places.

Laura's father and I sat down on opposite ends of a long sofa, in front of the fireplace. Her mother was in and out of the room, as if not knowing quite what to do with herself and trying to appear busy.

Laura, who had been standing, came toward the sofa. I wondered which one of us she would sit next to. When she seated herself beside her father, I tried to hold back a chuckle. I was definitely not disappointed and was actually relieved that we should have sat apart because I never, ever gave any display of affection or emotion in the presence of a girl's parents.

It wasn't any big secret that Laura's parents were not altogether thrilled about me. I tried to understand how they felt, these wealthy people living in an exclusive suburban town in Middle America. There I was, with this dark, Middle Eastern face and a foreign accent, dating their daughter. I could imagine that many an argument as to my suitability had preceded my arrival. This impression was reinforced as I continued to observe the couple's behavior during that visit. After the father's inquiry about my eating habits, he said absolutely nothing, even to his wife. The pair just looked at each other. I think I was the only one who felt really comfortable.

Laura took me on a tour of the house. I had never been in one that large or lavish. How different it was from my own family's unpretentious apartment. How dissimilar Laura's childhood must have been from mine. I tried to visualize current daily life in that setting.

The bathroom was huge and spotless. As I studied myself in the mirror and combed my hair, I realized that I was shedding. Determined to leave the bathroom as clean and shiny as I had found it, I used moistened toilet paper to account for every hair. It could be that my hair was always shedding that much, and that I first had to be in a rich bald man's pristine bathroom in order finally to become aware of my "affliction". I had always liked my hair and had taken good care of it. Now, at long last, I came to see that feature, as well as the rest of me, through Laura's parents' eyes. I was a shifty, dark foreigner with wild, unkempt, curly hair. I spoke the wrong language, ate the wrong foods, and was probably a savage and a rapist to boot. How much of this they actually felt I didn't know, of course, but I thought it significant that these ideas about myself had never before, in all my life, entered my head.

When the household retired for the night, I felt good to bed down in a comfortable private room, not having slept well in several days because of my long bus ride.

In the middle of the night Laura entered my room.

I had not had actual sexual intercourse since the very day I contracted herpes. I had learned that a carrier could not communicate the disease unless he had an active case at the time of sexual contact. Not having broken out in blisters since those I'd discovered in Shuli's house, I decided that now was the time to relieve myself of nearly a year's worth of desire. I would make love to Laura with all the passion imprisoned in my starving heart.

Laura removed her night clothes and stood naked beside my bed. We held hands, and, as she settled down next to me, talked softly about the past six months.

Her body looked different. I knew she had slept with at least a few men since leaving Israel, the denials in her letters notwithstanding. I brought up the subject.

"Oh, please," she begged, "don't ask me that."

But I insisted, and she admitted having had several men.

The annoyance I experienced at Laura's admission abated when she pointed out that my affair with Barbara while I was living with her hardly entitled me to saddle anyone with a chastity belt. Of course I had to agree, and I felt remorseful for having been judgmental of her behavior and even for having pushed her into revealing what she clearly wished to leave within her private realm of awareness.

But I had my own, very personal reason for agonizing over her revelation. I was not just a possessive lover. The truth is I might as well have suffered from impotence for all the competition I was able to muster against other men who took a liking to Laura. They were doing the work for me.

No matter. This was behind me. Laura would make love to me tonight. I was the one she most wanted. And it was going to be beautiful for both of us.

She moved closer to me. I kissed her and ran my hands slowly over her body.

Our desire about to be fulfilled, I made the cursed, dreaded discovery of blisters. A lump came to my throat, and my eyes became moist, but I wasn't about to cry. Rather my impulse was to scream to the sky and to curse the heavens until my throat bled me dry. In my mind I threw the tables over, smashed the lamps against the wall, and hurled everything in sight across the room. Then I came to myself, and, of course, everything was in place, but my face and my pillow were wet with tears.

Always it seemed, herpes came at the wrong time for whatever my designs — sexual or non-sexual. If I couldn't change the pattern of my herpes, at least I could alter my plans so as to escape the need and the hurt. We can't control what we want, ony what we do. In deciding to pack my bags and to leave, I was declaring to myself that I still had some say in my fate. The passivity entailed in remaining in Laura's house for the week which I had contemplated would have conflicted unbearably with my need to show my body who was boss. After two days of plastic living and two lonely, loveless nights, I was once again saying good-bye in an airport.

Laura drove me there for a flight to San Francisco, a city I'd wanted very much to see, but hadn't expected to visit quite this soon. We went through the familiar, tearful good-bye, and I was off. Although I knew I'd see Laura again before long, saying good-bye always turned out to be a frightfully sad thing to do.

Laura, Laura, Laura, I thought as we taxied down the runway, *do you really love me? Or are you just disappointed that I can't perform?* I asked myself whether love between men and women could ever be so unselfish and pure that the absence of sex would not cause disappointment. Was sex not, after all, the means by which the feelings of tenderness and joy in the presence of the beloved are most deliciously heightened? Why, then, did I think about Laura as if the existence of her disappointment and frustration reduced me to the status of a stud animal? It was not that I had ever professed undying love for Laura, but I did have to face the fact that, in being confronted by my most recent outbreak of blisters, I had hardly taken note of Laura's anguish, so absorbed had I been in my own.

As I continued with this train of thought, I realized that it wasn't getting me anywhere as far as sorting out my own feelings was concerned. If I could reach any conclusion, it was only that Laura might well have loved me.

The plane droned on, and my attention switched from my immediate past to the city that I was about to visit. In San Francisco I was to relish the anonymity that comes with being completely alone in a strange, new location.

As much as I had expected to like San Francisco, I did like it. I almost thought of it as the Jerusalem of the West, not that it bore any structural resemblance to the city of my dreams. Rather the similarity lay in the uncommonly intense power of both municipalities to intoxicate me with the essence of life.

I would spend hours by the ocean, gazing at the Golden Gate Bridge and listening to the fog horns, the seals and sea gulls, the gently lapping waves, and the busy city noises, each touching a different heart string, and all blending together in a subdued romantic splendor that shook me with some awesome force and transported me away from my wretched, mundane concerns. In that magnificent aloneness, my spirit gladdened by a veritable rhapsody of sound and color, I fancied sharing it all with someone who could cherish it as I did. Even in my solitude I prayed that these overpowering sensations would go on forever.

But nothing goes on forever, not even life itself. After a while the law of diminishing returns began to set in. To have thought it could be otherwise would have been expecting life always to be lived at a climactic pitch. When climax is forever, the very concept becomes meaningless, joyless, and unattainable. I started to sense how far I was from the familiar.

As if in defiance of my passionate soul, I grew to think of Laura more and more. Although she lacked the depth of spirit to cherish much of what I held dear, she seemed my only link with what was comfortable and known in those very lonesome days. How far could Boulder, Colorado, be from San Francisco? I was seeing the places I'd intended to see, but my itinerary, if you could call it that, was pulling me along at a rate I had not anticipated and, indeed, could hardly believe. I realized that only in contentment can one afford the luxury of holding still for a while. Since I could in no way count myself among the contented, I had to keep moving along. My five senses needed rapid changes of stimuli in order to prevent me from dwelling deeply on my situation. On I flew to Colorado.

8   *Marriage on the Rocks*

The flight to Denver gave me a chance to think about lighter matters than those I'd considered at San Francisco Bay. Mainly I reminisced about my days on the campus in Jerusalem, where, through Laura, I'd met a very interesting pair of women, Eleanor and Kathy.

Kathy was one of the students I had counseled, and Eleanor, who had gone to Jerusalem to visit her, was her mother. They, Laura, and I had been good friends there, Laura having known them from before in Boulder. I was particularly fond of Eleanor and used to enjoy chatting with her about all sorts of things. I tried to imagine how it would be for all four of us to get together again.

When finally I arrived in Boulder, I judged that it must be one of the most beautiful places in America. Here was a youthful college town set amidst the magnificent Rocky Mountains. It did not quite bring to mind any locale I had ever seen. Perhaps I would take an extended stay here. While Laura was studying, I could savor the majesty and serenity with which nature had endowed this place. I caught myself, here, as in San Francisco, in the unsettling confrontation with the fact that I could never share with Laura anything that had the power to move me to tears.

Laura shared an apartment with Nancy, a Japanese-American from Hawaii, and I became, for a while, the third member of the household. Nancy did not make me feel any more welcome than Laura's parents had.

A writer and a photographer, she was quiet, interesting, serious, and intelligent. I probably would have liked her and relished trading ideas with her if not for the circumstances of our acquaintance. For one thing, to my chagrin, Laura had told her about my herpes. Her awareness of it, I thought, might have accounted for her never looking me straight in the eye. Another cause of my discomfort with Nancy stemmed from the inaccessibility of the bathroom to her, except through the bedroom that I shared with Laura. Neither Nancy nor I felt at all comfortable about her having to pass by us in bed. By contrast, Laura didn't appear the least bit disturbed.

Laura, I was to learn, tended to make light of my not fitting in with her family and friends. Actually she moved through daily life all but oblivious to my relations with those whom we hadn't known together in Jerusalem. I grew to see a new side of her. To know the same old person in an altogether different setting is to know that person in a brand new way. As I watched Laura relate to her various friends during the first few days of my stay, and, as I saw her in contrast to some of them, notably Nancy, I came to think of her as some kind of dummy and wondered why I had never previously observed what now seemed as clear as the crisp mountain air of that January.

Everything she did I would see in terms of poor judgment or deficient intelligence. She didn't excel in her studies and displayed immeasurably less productivity in her work than Nancy.

I was particularly bothered by a story she told me, Nancy, and another young woman. In traveling from the airport to her apartment she'd befriended a young man and invited him to spend the night there. Upon awakening in the morning, she discovered both the man and her money and jewelry to be gone. How on earth, I thought, could she have invited a perfect stranger to stay overnight? And, having survived that colossal blunder, how could she so proudly and glibly, and with such obvious relish, be relating this story to us? Had she not emerged any the wiser from what should have been a very humbling learning experience.?

Another thing that disturbed me greatly about Laura was her marijuana smoking. She had taken up this habit, I learned, shortly after leaving Israel. I found the whole drug scene abhorrent and did not mince words with her in making my feelings plain. We had some very bitter arguments over this habit, but it didn't drive me away from her.

How potent a force the *status quo* had always been in my life, and, with my herpes, I could ill afford to treat the *status quo* with less than my usual apparent reverence for it. I surely did not have any more regard for Laura than I'd had in Jerusalem. We argued incessantly about marijuana; about what I regarded as her unwarranted revelations about me to her parents and friends; about her clothing, which I saw as unflattering for her proportions; and about a host of less consequential matters. But I stayed on. The thought of clinging to her even a trifle less tenaciously filled me with fear. I don't know whether I even realized then the extent of my fear, so unaccustomed was I to deciding what I did and didn't want.

Holding on to Laura as I did brought me quite naturally my first real sex act since contracting herpes almost a year before. I had thought that my reentry to the world of sexuality would be in Kansas City, but my condition there postponed it for a month.

An integral part of the fabric of my relationship with Laura was, simply put, that sex with her was no great pleasure either physically or emotionally. Somehow, I thought, this first time would be different. After nearly a whole year, sex would be glorious with anyone.

The experience turned out to be merely all right. It certainly relieved me of an accumulation of practically unbearable sexual tension, but it did no more than that.

I had never told Laura of my most intimate feelings during sex with her. What would have been the point of hurting her, especially for something she couldn't change? The fact was that, despite the sweet lips, the heavenly scent of perfume, and the delightful breasts, she was not desirable. The ultimate act itself made me think of what it must feel like to masturbate with two stones. Her vagina was so large that I felt constantly on the hunt for a bit of warm, juicy flesh to snuggle into. The chronic dryness used to make me think that Laura was never sufficiently aroused. Yet I knew this was not the case.

So there I was, living with a girl who was undesirable to me in numerous ways. The more I stayed with Laura, the more I felt like an automaton. I grew decreasingly fond of myself and increasingly disgusted by my deficiency in being able to decide what was right for me.

One of the most incredible decisions of my life was made for me only a few days after my arrival in Boulder. I became very ill from a severely infected tooth. The local dentist advised me in no uncertain terms to have surgery performed immediately. My aching head filled up with all sorts of confusing, painful thoughts, hardly the least pressing of which was how to pay the two hundred seventy-five dollars required for the operation. To complicate matters further, Eleanor and Kathy had invited Laura and me to spend the weekend in their apartment some forty miles away. I was extremely eager to see them and did not wish to become involved with a series of postponements. In America, I had found, visiting was not done on a spur-of-the-moment basis, as it was in Israel.

Laura took care of the financial problem by giving me the money for the surgery. In so doing she created a far bigger problem for me than she ever solved. But I was not to know this until later. If my dental difficulties had occurred in San Francisco or in some other place where I had no friends, I could have asked Gilda or some other relative to wire me the needed funds, and would not have felt indebted, nor would I have sensed my dignity and my defenses to be slowly ebbing away.

As it was, Laura, through no fault of her own, robbed me of my pride and, at the same time, lavished me with love. Despite my own ambiguous feelings, I really did catch the flame of her devotion radiating clear through to my heart.

I underwent my surgery, and we kept our appointment with Eleanor and Kathy. But the aftermath of the operation and the excitement of seeing them again, not to mention the confusion generated by the presence of several other female friends off and on during those few days, made for a less than idyllic visit. The low oxygen at that altitude made me feel dizzy, tired, and sick. The vivid red of the walls, the floor, the bedding, and practically everything else in the Japanese-style room that I occupied aggravated my misery. Despite my efforts to be sociable, I ended up spending many hours in bed, taking the antibiotics prescribed by the dentist. I could scarcely pick myself up, and Laura made it so that I wouldn't have to. Like Florence Nightingale she took care of my every need. How I felt her kindness, and what a deadly kindness it was. But who could ever have suspected it at the time? For Laura and the others it was all very simple. I was sick, and she was treating me with tender loving care. What could have been more natural? For me, however, it was quite different, more so than I could have begun to understand even had I been more lucid.

In one of my dizzier moments I mumbled to Laura, "You're so good and kind to me I would marry you."

Without a moment's hesitation she ran downstairs to tell the other women the *news*. Hardly a minute later Eleanor excitedly entered the room where I lay in what seemed to me a semi-comatose state. She could barely believe that I'd finally proposed marriage to Laura.

"Yes," I said, "she's one of the best, and I love her."

Even from my bed it wasn't difficult to detect a minor riot emanating from the other women, who were with Laura downstairs.

By some quirk of fate, Laura's parents, aware that she was spending the weekend there, phoned just as I was responding to Eleanor, who, from the extension next to my bed, broke the news to them.

I was falling in deeper and deeper and didn't know what to do. Matters were getting out of hand. Was I in my right mind? Were the women in that house in their right minds to have taken seriously the utterances of a man who, while not actually semi-comatose, was certainly not altogether coherent?

Downstairs Laura rushed to pick up the extension and conversed joyfully. From what I could hear it was evident that her parents were confused. They weren't the only ones. From where I lay I could hear her mother crying. She sounded happy, but I wasn't convinced. Her father struck me as being deeply concerned, and I hoped that his sobriety would catch on to Laura.

I hoped, and I didn't hope. Undoubtedly some part of me had wanted all this and had pushed me into that stuporous proposal. The part of me that hadn't wanted this marriage, namely the heart, the brain, and the libido, now lay immersed in an agony of fear, hopelessness, and resignation. Once again I had bowed to a decision made for me by forces I wasn't controlling.

Lest I should lose all self-respect, I hastened to try to convince myself that, as a herpes sufferer, I had every reason to be glad that a comfortable, familiar woman loved me and eagerly anticipated marrying me.

When she hung up the phone, she threw her arms around me and fairly squealed, "We're getting married!"

On the following day Laura set about making actual wedding arrangements. Wasting no time, she called the court to set a date. The one say I had in the matter was to veto her choice of Saturday, February 14, in favor of the thirteenth. I had no objections to Valentine's Day, but holding our wedding on the Sabbath did not strike me right since Jewish weddings are never performed then. And getting married on Friday, the thirteenth, did not seem to me any more ominous than tying the knot on any other day.

Besides Laura's taking an RH blood test and our inviting several of our local friends to be present, there remained frighteningly little to do, and the wedding date was rushing to meet us.

I had very little time to feel anything, and it was probably better that way because what I did feel wasn't good. Maybe life requires a person to pass through a tunnel of doubt, terror, and despair before taking any major step forward. But why didn't anyone else I had ever observed seem to have passed through that tunnel? Did people keep their misgivings to themselves so much that one's own were the only ones of which a person ever knew? I wondered whether convicts on death row felt as I did. In entering a relationship which should have epitomized the closeness of two souls, I was incongruously alone, and everything was moving away from me in all directions, with alarming speed, as in the *big bang* theory of creation.

Damn it all! Why did it hurt so much just to be alive?

On the actual date of the wedding, barely a few weeks after my memorable *proposal*, I bravely faced the music. According to the photos I saw afterwards I was even smiling. Aren't people supposed to smile at their weddings? I was doing everything precisely as I had always been programmed, but the program was not of my making.

We had to wait for the judge, who was then at a hearing on a murder case. My business there, I thought, didn't differ significantly in gravity from what his honor was then tending to. When he came out, we shook hands. Laura and I signed the necessary papers. We held hands, and he performed the ceremony. It was over.

But of course it wasn't over; it was just beginning. Within only a few minutes I was courageous enough to acknowledge to myself the feeling I'd had all along, namely that I was relinquishing my freedom. As we rode away from the court house, I saw many young girls. Perhaps I could never have had them anyway, but, at least, up to that point, I had been able to know the deliciousness of hope. Now that precious freedom that allowed me to experience hope had vanished. I was trapped in the worst way, no longer just by herpes, but by Laura as well.

The next morning I awoke to a very gloomy day. Although it was

Valentine's Day, I didn't feel or anticipate feeling much love. While Laura slept, I arose from bed, walked to the window, and gazed dejectedly out. Laura lay there snoring. My stomach was knotted up. I looked at her briefly and then returned my attention to the out of doors. I was trying to escape. Something about Laura sickened me. As she lay in bed heaving and snoring, she reminded me of a hibernating bear. Although my height exceeded hers by several inches, the sight of her, even more than of the sweeping gray clouds and the huge mountains and boulders of the Rockies, made me feel small.

I thought of how unhappy we really were. I, for sure, was unhappy, but Laura too, for all the satisfaction she was experiencing at having bagged her catch, was not genuinely content. Most of the time we were unable to make love. As I dared to think about the future, I could see that I didn't have the kind of response I wanted from a life partner. I didn't see how we could ever be intimate as long as she continued to discuss our personal business with her mother, Nancy, Eleanor, and a few other friends. This practice continued despite my protests.

I returned to bed and lay down next to the bear. While she slept, I thought more about the future. We had discussed the possibility of my going off to New York to take David up on his offer of employment. It struck me that it might be worth my while to spend some time in earning money while Laura was studying. I seemed to be in her way anyhow as I believed that my presence in Boulder distracted her to the point where her grades were suffering.

Laura, however, did not look favorably upon this idea, and, so, I decided to postpone discussing it for the time being.

I became aware of my intense discomfort with our bed. My unhappiness on that day magnified all my petty annoyances. Laura's weight, I lamented, increased the bed's tendency to sag in the middle. I had been awakening every morning with a back ache from that damnable bed.

My mind went wandering again. This time my thoughts turned to Nancy. Here was yet another person about whom I had ambiguous feelings. While I strongly sensed that she did not care for either Laura or me, I was finding it less and less difficult to converse with her. That she understood what I had to say should have pleased me, perhaps, but instead it merely increased my anxiety by reminding me of how poor my new bride and I were at communicating. Nancy, with her positive, productive attitude, reminded me, to my discomfort, of how I had been at an earlier, less troubled stage of my life.

Laura put her leg on my stomach. This habit of hers was growing increasingly intolerable. I would sooner have slept under the weight of a fallen tree trunk. Abandoning the possibility of sleeping, I arose from bed again and paced around the room, gazing idly through the window and wondering whether Nancy had any ideas of what was going on.

I kept comparing Laura with Nancy. I thought about the antagonism that existed all around in our ménage à trois. I found its most intense presence in my relationship with Laura. I wondered how it could be that neither of us had backed down from our wedding plans despite the silent rage growing between us during the weeks leading up to that Friday, the thirteenth. The hostility that Nancy felt emanated from her continually being thrown in the midst of arguments between Laura and me, as well, I'm sure, as from my being in the apartment in the first place. I was a factor she had not counted on when agreeing to room with Laura.

Only in my parents' home, after the completion of my job in Jerusalem, had I known as much antipathy toward myself as I was now experiencing, and this time the feeling stemmed from my herpes only to the extent that, without it, I would never have married Laura.

At a later time I found it interesting to speculate about what my feeling toward Laura, herpes, and the future would have been if Nancy had not been in our lives, if everything except Nancy's existence, or a least her presence in that apartment, had been as it actually was. All of her positive qualities sharply contrasted with those of Laura, who was neither smart nor industrious, neither sincere nor discreet. And, in reminding me of my former, irretrievable self, Nancy unsuspectingly banished my chances of building a new me with the positive building blocks that I had been attempting to amass from the rubble. In addition, Nancy's hostility produced in me a defensiveness that drained me of some of the psychic energy which I otherwise would have earmarked for solving the problems of my relationship with Laura, my job situation, and my herpes.

Nancy actually symbolized an opposite kind of life to what I had been living. I didn't feel like myself anymore. How far I had come from that person I used to be. But I couldn't put my finger on just what was missing.

Somehow it was important for me to talk with Nancy. Yet she often clammed up just when I most needed her companionship, and her silence gave her a mysterious aura. Sometimes I felt like exploding at her. At these times I thought of myself as a Hawaiian volcano. She reminded me of the early Chinese settlers in Hawaii, who persevered despite adversity. I decided that I, too, would not give up.

As the weeks wore on after our wedding, things started to get worse with Laura, at least from my point of view. The studying she did for her upcoming exams triggered many explosive arguments between us, not exclusively about the studying itself. After spending the whole day reviewing her lessons in the library, she would return to the apartment to join me. If not for my presence, she would have spent her evenings unwinding at the various party-like activities that always seemed to be going on around the campus. If I had been inclined differently, the obvious thing to do would have been for us to go off partying together. However, with many of the people with whom Laura enjoyed letting her hair down, I didn't have the greatest rapport. Although it was terribly important to me that Laura should finish her scholastic endeavors successfully, I could see easily that the discord caused by the divergence of our evening interests had only the most deleterious effect on her academically.

We lived in two different worlds. For either of us to have given in, even a little, would have caused that person's demise as a distinct, worthy human creature. For me the ideal sharing of a segment of time with another person consisted of in-depth, philosophical conversation, the drinking in of nature's beauty, and involvement in off-beat fun activities that lent themselves to lighthearted, carefree laughter, the kind that always brought to mind the advice of my religious friend, who counseled that diversion purifies the soul. As for Laura, her idea of a good time was a bull session, smoking marijuana, and getting drunk.

Maybe the comparison between us lacks fairness and objectivity, being made, as it is, by one of us. But that really doesn't matter because it demonstrates anyway how truly far apart we were. I can state for a fact that my vision of Laura as a shallow, irresponsible, indiscreet, overweight, tactless, myopic dummy was matched by her vision of me as a stuffy, glum, critical, secretive, jobless killjoy. Since personal qualities exist in people only in relation to other people, it's pointless to consider whether either of us actually behaved as the other claimed. Our arguments were for naught. We simply had two different approaches to life, and neither of us could admit their irreconcilability.

Just as Laura and I occupied two different worlds, she had two worlds all to herself — one consisting of her studies and the other of her life with me. It was clear that the latter was infringing on the former.

I considered more and more seriously working in New York. I wanted to leave Laura free to study, unhindered by the negative feelings our arguing engendered. I also craved doing away with my being at loose ends, and of course the prospect of having money to put aside for the future played a formidable role in propelling me into what I did next.

I would have been willing to take on almost any kind of a job. But, as I mulled over the possibilities, I decided that my best avenue of approach lay in my acceptance of employment with David in New York. Although Laura opposed this plan, I phoned him anyway. I reasoned that, if he made me an attractive offer, the plan would become more palatable to Laura. On the other hand, if his offer proved unappealing, I myself would lose interest, and the matter would be closed.

When I called David, however, I received a bit of a surprise. Instead of even discussing the terms of my possible employment at one of his stores, he announced that he wanted to visit me. It was like David to come up with something out of left field in that way, but quite unlike him to travel. I told him I'd be happy to see him and spent the next few days very much looking forward to his visit.

That Friday morning Eleanor drove me to Denver to fetch David from the airport. During our twenty-five-mile ride back to Boulder, his enthusiasm knew no bounds. This was his first trip out of the New York area since his arrival in the States. His dynamic, ambitious nature had kept him working straight through these five years in his stores, never once pausing for the refreshment of a vacation. He expressed surprise at the scenery, the pace, and the apparently variant ways of life in different parts of the country. The people he observed all the way from the airport to our apartment building struck him, he said, as being very slow and mellow.

I introduced him to Laura. He behaved in a very courtly manner toward her, and they engaged in some pleasant small talk. As I watched them converse, I wondered what they thought of each other, particularly how David viewed Laura. His unexpectedly courteous demeanor toward her made me feel that he liked her, but it didn't take him awfully long to make his true feelings known to me.

David and I went downstairs and outside, two old friends wanting to catch up on the news since their last meeting.

"What do you think about my wife?" I asked him, extremely eager to learn his opinion of Laura.

"No good, no good!" came the reply, hurled at me with dizzying speed. A bit thrown, I didn't respond to this dictum. David wasn't looking for a response; in his usual glib way he was simply telling me exactly what was on his mind. He said, by way of explanation, that he was shocked I would even date, much less marry, a woman of such large proportions.

The subject changed, and not a moment too soon, as far as I was concerned. We turned our attention to plans for the evening. Ever since learning that my New York friend was soon to arrive, Eleanor had expressed interest in fixing Kathy up with him. We had discussed the matter in the car en route from Denver, and David had appeared quite eager. We now decided to invite the mother and daughter out to eat that evening.

True to form David announced that he would be treating us all to dinner, and he made sure to select the most sumptuous restaurant in the area. Privately he had declared his determination to show me how to make American girls go crazy. He was going to teach me a memorable lesson to the effect that money talks more loudly than anything else. No one could ever say he didn't try. He shamelessly and vocally ordered crab meat and other expensive delicacies for everyone, as well as three bottles of champagne, easily spending at least two hundred dollars. To me his attempts to impress everyone with his wealth, power, and sophistication were so blatantly transparent as to be embarrassing. But apparently not everyone thinks like me. I became uncomfortably and alarmingly convinced of the power of money when I saw Kathy kissing him repeatedly. Tall, beautiful Kathy was falling easily into David's hands. How could she have known that she was only a part of a demonstration staged for my benefit? The ease with which she fell into his trap surprised even David.

The sight of Kathy's publicly kissing a man she had just met, even as she spoke to him of her boyfriend out of town, upset Eleanor to the point where she left the restaurant in the middle of the meal. David became insulted.

The meal broke up in a turbulent argument, with David claiming that Eleanor didn't like him and my urging him to keep his feelings toward her to himself.

After dropping Laura and Kathy off, I drove David to his motel, where we continued the argument about dinnertime events.

I remained there until late that night, and we discussed a variety of topics, none of the others as far reaching as his offer to me of a job for five hundred dollars a week.

Again I considered how staying on with Laura might undermine her chances to get her Bachelor's degree. Maybe underneath it all I was rationalizing my desire to get away from Laura, although I also felt pangs of guilt about having been hard on her. But, regardless of how I rearranged the facts of our situation, I still felt like a distraction.

Suddenly I told David I'd accept his offer. It was, oddly enough, the thought of Nancy's dissatisfaction with our living arrangement that pushed me to this decision. Unexpectedly my mind's eye was seized by an image of her disapproving face.

Perhaps I behaved naively, but it was very difficult to find work in Colorado, and David's offer frankly tempted me.

9 *Cesspool of Hell*

Just before I left Boulder for Denver several weeks later, Laura and I tearfully said good-bye. As she walked away from my slowly moving bus, wearing that pretty white dress, I watched her until she disappeared from view. I remember feeling both love and pity for her. In those moments I knew that, in some way, this good-bye would be forever.

My Trailways bus left Denver at night. As I boarded it, I had an intensely heavy, negative feeling. Laura wasn't thrilled by what I was doing. I, myself, had to face the fact that I wasn't entirely sold on my course of action. Sometimes I got the impression from the turns my life was taking that, no matter what I might have decided at any given point, I would have been wrong. At this particular juncture, going off to New York didn't excite me. I felt distinctly alone and actually terrified of what lay ahead. My already shaky marriage might not survive a prolonged separation. Furthermore, my recollections of Forty-Second Street, which was where David intended to station me, depressed me terribly. What was I getting myself into? I sat alone in the bus. Although, in fact, I had various seat mates along the way, I was very much living inside myself, and all the doors were tightly shut.

My immediate plans consisted of heading to Boston via a rather circuitous route. I would visit Gilda's family and then make my way south to New York. I had promised myself a rain check for Boston when it warmed up, and, although March offered no more hope of warmth than December, I was eagerly on my way.

My route took me first to Chicago, where, I had decided, I would break up my trip. I had already traveled two nights and one day.

I arrived early in the morning and spent the whole day walking around. Keeping on the move helped take my mind off of the disagreeably raw, cold weather.

Toward evening I sought refuge in an art museum, which seemed the only warm, safe place around. Thoroughly exhausted, I nearly collapsed into a chair and fell asleep. I kept awakening and dozing as art lovers bustled around me. Each time I opened my eyes I observed people staring at me. I felt like one of the statues. Something about this experience underscored my feeling of aloneness and of not quite belonging anywhere.

After dark I boarded another bus and rode all night, headed for Buffalo.

My fellow passengers impressed me as being the real people of America. In spite of the fact that many of them seemed weird and miserable, I liked them. Their simplicity and genuineness brought a certain measure of warmth and cheer to the cold, weary, lonely traveler that I was.

I arrived in Buffalo around noon and was immediately struck by the fierceness of the cold weather. Extreme weather conditions never looked favorably upon my blisters, and I was concerned lest my condition be aggravated. I was determined, however, not to allow the elements to prevent me from seeing Niagara Falls. Accordingly, I took another bus and arrived in the midst of what was surely the cloudiest, rainiest, coldest, gloomiest day I had ever experienced. The unexpected sight of the wondrous falls frozen into near stillness seemed to stop the already slow, sad beat of my heart, which was itself frozen in more ways than one. But, just as I noticed that the flow had not stopped completely, I once again saw myself as being able to go on despite the heaviness of my burden. Yes, I comforted myself, like the plants thriving in the dryness of the desert, like the Chinese settlers facing adversity in Hawaii, and like Niagara Falls in the frozen winter, I, too, would go on, and I would some day rise above all my suffering and be happy again.

As I walked through the town of Niagara Falls, on the New York side, I thought it strange that I was apparently the only tourist around. It seemed to me that I was forever out of step.

I came upon some teenagers, who asked me where I was from. When I replied, "Israel," they said they'd never heard of that place. In such cold weather, I thought, who can study?

I bussed on to Boston that night and spent a few uneventful days with Gilda.

In getting the 4:30 p.m. train that I'd decided to ride to New York, I first had to take the subway from Brookline into Boston. In the subway train I ran into a friend of Gilda's. This girl had the distinct impression that we had not allowed ourselves sufficient time to make the connection with ease. It didn't take me long to see that she knew what she was talking about.

At the station in Boston I waited with her as she paid her fare to New York with a credit card. I, of course, had paid in cash.

I rushed after her toward the train. She just managed to catch it. It began to move exactly as I reached it and stepped on with one foot. And I would have succeeded in boarding if the conductor had not practically pushed me off. If only he had stepped out of the way or taken my hand, I could have made it with ease. Instead he just stood there blocking my way and telling me that I wouldn't make it.

This man *was* the train, it occurred to me in a blur of goings-on around my head. If not for that iron giant, he would have had no stature whatsoever. All the qualities which one might attribute to a train, he lacked as an individual, I was convinced. The power, the speed, and the enormity, he internalized to the extent that he became qualified and authorized to reject me on behalf of his well endowed senior partner. I was not fast enough, strong enough, or big enough to get aboard successfully. The other passengers had at least humbled themselves to the point of boarding more promptly and soberly than I. In his mind I had challenged the train and was, of course, destined to come out second best.

At any rate, his words became a self-fulfilling prophecy as I lost my balance and fell to the platform. As the train roared away, I lay there dazed. A nearby laborer asked whether I was all right. After a few moments I arose — shaken, but alive and well. If the fall had been at a slightly different angle, I might well have slid down onto the tracks. The greatness of man, I thought, is not that he never falls, but that he can stand up after a fall.

I had to wait an hour for the next train. This one I boarded in a more conventional, leisurely fashion. I just wanted to work hard so that I could save up some money for the future. With this thought the principal occupant of my mind, I commenced my four-hour journey to the Big Apple.

I sat down not far from a group of talkative college students. For the greater part of an hour I listened to them rant on about all kinds of pseudo-intellectual matters. I judged that they thought themselves quite smart and that they enjoyed matching wits. As far as I was concerned, however, they were lacking in original thinking. They appeared to be parroting what they'd heard in class instead of speaking from genuine conviction, the kind arrived at through voluminous life experience, of which I gathered they hadn't tasted very deeply.

Having heard enough of their chatter, I picked myself up and headed for the dining car, where I sat down next to a pretty young girl. We struck up a pleasant conversation and spent several hours going over a whole array of interesting subjects, both light and heavy. I could see that she found me attractive and that she was eager to further our relationship.

What gnawed away at my peace of mind was that I felt desire for her. Here I was, married for one month, and already thinking of how delightful it was to be conversing with this new friend. Naturally more alarming than my mere enjoyment of the conversation were the signals my body was sending out to me about how pleasurable it would be to embrace this lovely stranger.

In having all these feelings, I saw myself as being dishonest; I was a traitor in my thoughts. Was this an odd feeling for a man who had considerably less than the expected amount of love and admiration for his wife? Maybe, but that was how I felt, and, whether surprising or not, the feeling ate away at me. It behaved like a growth in my mind and seemed to sprout tentacles, which choked off my other feelings and thoughts and gave me no peace.

The milieu I was to enter did not contribute in any way to the promotion of a more peaceful mental state.

From Penn Station I exited into a different, dynamic world. Although this was not my first time in New York, I felt as if it were, as if my earlier series of visits had been just a travelogue, which couldn't begin to prepare me for what lay ahead. Even near Penn Station I sensed danger, and I knew I was headed for worse.

It was Friday afternoon, and I was as tired as if it had been much later. I took a taxi to David's store on Forty-Second Street, where I found my friend busily working. Knowing David as well as I did, and knowing that he knew me as well as he did, I should not have been surprised when he began to assign me tasks almost before I had put down my luggage.

I did begin to work immediately. I was thoroughly prepared for hard work and not the least upset by David's giving it to me. On Forty-Second Street drudgery is probably the least upsetting entity one encounters.

Even in what little was left of that Friday, this famous street opened my eyes to its darkest secrets. As I transferred cartons between the store and the street, and, as I dealt with customers inside, I could see that I had landed in a crazy world. Poverty, I had seen and known, but this was ingrained poverty, poverty without nobility. I was no stranger to the sight of unclean living conditions, but here there seemed not a breath of hope or even knowledge of something better. Laura's marijuana smoking seemed child's play when compared to the drug dealing here. The buying, selling, pushing, and using of every imaginable body-damaging drug were facts of life to which one accustomed oneself. Thievery, likewise, was rampant. One had to live by the assumption that everyone around was out to steal in one form or another — shoplifting, pickpocketing, mugging, purse snatching, holding up a store — the sky was the limit. What would have constituted paranoia elsewhere was merely realism on Forty-Second Street. It became clear right off that I had unwittingly traded one depressing reality for another.

That night, as quitting time mercifully came to my rescue, David drove me home in his gray Mercedes, accompanied by his girlfriend Karlene, a former beauty queen. The contrast between the depravity of Forty-Second Street and the opulence of David's penthouse bewildered me to the point where I could well have done without the experiences of the ride between them.

Karlene sat next to David, and I occupied the back seat. I didn't have the best impression of her, except that she was very beautiful. My image of New York girls — no doubt overgeneralized, but my image nevertheless — was that of ingrained superficiality and unbecoming enthusiasm for money. For David's part, he was only too happy, it seemed, to impress her with his wealth, as he had done with Kathy in Colorado. He catered to her every demand. It was difficult to tell which of them was deriving more from this symbiotic relationship. Each was putting on a grand show for the other.

Karlene asked me what my profession was. I replied that I was an agronomist. She went on to ask what I was doing in New York, and I explained my intention to earn some money for the future. She seemed uncomfortable.

David's life style and value system certainly lent themselves to the way things seemed to be set up in New York. All you needed to live the great life was money; the girls and the good times would follow automatically. Within the next few days I became convinced that David had everything money could buy — material possessions and salable people.

Among the material possessions was a second car, an open sports car. A few days after my arrival, David, Karlene, and I got into it; she drove. From the back seat I looked at the big city — all around me and straight up. The radio played "New York, New York". The experience was like something out of a movie. Yes, I thought, rewriting somewhat the song's lyrics, if David can make it here, anyone can. I included myself, of course, and actually felt a glimmer of optimism enter my gloomy world.

Indeed I was starting to enjoy my tour. The ride was exciting and filled with surprises. I didn't care that my companions were trying to bolster their egos by showing me around. I enjoyed myself in spite of them.

Each day, six or seven days a week, I would work long hours in the store, from nine to midnight, and return afterwards to David's apartment to unwind. During that time David would receive many phone calls from women — all superficial types, as far as I could judge from his end of the conversations. He used to give them handsome, though poorly functioning, watches. This kept them coming back to him.

David's love affair with money came into ever sharper focus. The pretty green paper for which I toiled every day flowed in and out of his hands in vast quantities as he made one deal after another. With his deals, as with his gambling ventures, sometimes he gained a lot, and sometimes he lost, but always the money flowed.

Meanwhile, I labored. I spent hours and hours working like a horse to start to build a future, which was uncertain at best. Whenever I compared David's aims with mine, I wondered how we could ever have become friends. Yet he was a fast friend. I truly believed he would give me the shirt off his back.

As I worked, I saw more and more of Forty-Second Street. Uneasily I discovered that one could grow accustomed to those unsavory surroundings — the filthy streets and unwashed people, the drunks, the whores, the sick of body and mind. I did not understand how people could sink to such a level of living, but there it was, and very little could have surprised me after a few days of immersion in it.

I recall one rainy day when I looked out and saw a preacher standing on a chair in the midst of this Sodom and Gomorrah. He preached hope to whoever would listen. How he dared to hope, I could not fathom. As he spoke, a man in his audience called out, accusing him of preaching only because his church was paying him. An argument ensued. I returned to my work.

I felt myself in a cesspool of hell. I witnessed stabbings every few days. The weeks wore on, and my initial confusion turned into a feeling of actually belonging. I was getting herpes every few weeks. Having it made me feel more a part of the life of the street. David knew of my herpes, and his knowledge intensified this feeling of belonging. Somehow, being on Forty-Second Street made me more content with my affliction. In a sense I felt I was with my own kind. All sorts of diseases came walking into David's store. I once even suspected I saw leprosy. How far I had come since passing the infirmary in Jerusalem! The parts of me which, in the beginning, seemed to have stayed in Israel and Colorado now belonged more to Forty-Second Street. I even felt safer.

I started to learn how a small business runs and became especially familiar with watches, radios, and other electronic devices. We were always guarding against shoplifting, and I became adept at preventing thievery too.

When I arrived in New York, I was a pretty gentle person, but, as the time passed, I found myself growing tough and actually feeling hatred toward some of the more violent, larcenous customers. I never shared my evolving feelings with David; there was no time.

One of the crudest practices I had occasion to witness centered around the clearly great popularity of oral sex among the habitués of the street. My introduction to this flourishing *business* occurred when a young woman entered the store and asked me whether I wanted a *b.j.* Thinking she was inquiring about our merchandise, I told her we didn't have any. When she said she wanted to sell it to me, I told her I wasn't interested. Overhearing us, one of my fellow workers, greatly amused by my ignorance, told me quietly that a *b.j.* stood for *blow job.* Thus were my eyes opened to yet another of Forty-Second Street's lowly activities.

The custom, at least as practiced in our store — and I'm certain we weren't the only practitioners — consisted of the selling of oral sex by young female locals to male employees. The employee would take the girl to the back room, where they would quickly engage in oral sex, for which his payment to her assumed the form of a supposedly reduced price for some electronic device or another. The price, however, was not actually reduced, but the unsuspecting woman never realized that she was paying every bit as much as any customer who never paid a visit to the back room.

When it came time to pay, I entered the picture since I often manned the cash register. I sank lower and lower as I came to see myself as a cashier in a whore house.

Some of my co-workers urged me to treat myself to a *b.j.*, but I never did — for two reasons, in addition to simply not finding the whole business very tempting. First, I didn't want to take the chance of giving herpes to any of the girls or, through them, to the other employees. Second, despite the less than ideal circumstances of my marriage, I still saw myself as a married man and regarded marital faithfulness as including sexual exclusivity. However, I now wonder how valid my reasons were. The existence of two reasons raises the question of how fervently I believed in either one.

I phoned Laura often, but avoided telling her of the seedier goings-on where I was. I didn't say that I was seeing things I never would have believed and that I felt I was becoming an animal. All Laura knew was that my life was hectic and exhausting. I also didn't tell her that I was turning into a different person — aggressive and frustrated. I wondered whether those qualities would manifest themselves when I returned to Boulder. Would I be yelling at Laura as I was now yelling at customers? I had never been a yeller, but here I was, relating to them in the only way that seemed, then and there, natural.

My chief joy at that time of my life was my nightly midnight shower in David's bathroom. The mildly hot water gently untied the knotted muscles of my neck, back, and arms. Whoever called oil liquid gold never knew the soothing, relaxing powers of hot water. My soul and I communicated during those heavenly showers. The water made love to me as it enveloped me tenderly with the warmth of its arms. It seemed to care for me like a lover. As it poured down in sheets over my eager body, it even moved like a lover.

I was myself again — restored and refreshed. Though making love with the shower water might have constituted a breach of faith with Laura, it was a splendid affirmation of faith with myself. I would not allow my feelings to die. To suppress one's most powerful feelings is to kill oneself a little bit.

As much as I enjoyed showering, I had to face the fact that I envied David for certain elements of his life style, which I perceived as nearly diametrically opposite to my own. I was poor and married, and I had herpes. He was rich, he was surrounded by girls, and he gave every indication of enjoying life to the fullest.

I often found myself losing out as a result of David's good times, not through envy alone. Many nights I couldn't sleep because of his sexual activities in the next room. "Deeper, deeper!" I frequently heard girls call out. Even at night I had no peace.

One Saturday David suggested we drive to Atlantic City for the evening. On the drive down we heard the song "The Gambler" on the radio. This put me in the mood. We took an expensive hotel room although we weren't at all sure whether we'd spend the night.

David started playing blackjack and lost eight thousand dollars in one hour. He was so upset that he insisted we return immediately to New York.

The ride was decidedly less than pleasant. David actually blamed me for bringing him bad luck. I had had my first lesson in gambling and its effects on people. America is a country which eats its residents, I concluded.

It was around this time that I decided to leave New York for Boulder. After about two months of violence, degradation, drudgery, and frustration, I had had enough.

Using some of the money I'd saved, I spent three more days and nights on a Greyhound bus, crossing most of America. Again I found myself enjoying the genuine, simple people who were my traveling companions.

10 *Fifteen Days of Laura*

When I reached Denver, some disturbing questions about my destiny entered my mind. I asked myself where I was and what I was doing. I felt far away from everything and everybody, as if I didn't belong anywhere. My heart raced as I came face to face with the reality of my disconnectedness. I had no roots anywhere, only widely scattered pieces of myself.

Arriving home in Boulder I just wanted to shower, make love, and sleep, probably in that order. I put down my luggage and hugged and kissed a very happy Laura.

After our lengthy separation it was only natural that we both should be longing for sex, but that same night, no doubt because of the wearisome bus ride, the herpes flared up again. Whoever hated me up there must have been rolling on the clouds in a fit of laughter.

For Laura and me, however, the inability to make love teased and frustrated us and wore away whatever good remained in our relationship. At first she tried to console me, but her bitter disappointment was evident.

In the days that followed, the tensions between us mounted, and our tempers grew shorter. People need sex. While food and air are absolute prerequisites for the maintenance of life, sex, for most of us, must be present too if that life is to hold any sweetness.

Laura's need became such that she soberly declared her willingness to get herpes from me — if only she once again could lose herself in that tenderest of joys.

I, however, was not ready to give her my disease, having established the firm policy of never engaging in sex unless I were absolutely free of herpes.

Herpes is generally far worse for a woman than for a man. For one thing, she can never be quite as nearly certain as he of when it's safe to have sex. Moreover her risk of cancer exceeds that of women without herpes, and her children must be delivered by caesarean section in order to avoid the contamination which would very likely accompany a normal delivery. I was certainly unwilling to have my children enter the world already infected with herpes.

Our frustrated sex life was not the only source of tension our marriage underwent. There were also the matters of Laura's marijuana smoking and her conversations with her mother and friends about me.

During my absence from Colorado she had smoked marijuana despite her earlier promises to stay away from it. Upon my return I happened upon the stuff, and Laura was cornered into admitting she'd indulged herself. Regardless of the relative merits of our respective positions, I surely did not help matters any by calling Laura a "parasite" although I trust it would not be difficult for anyone to see how I'd come to regard her as such. Learning what she'd done was like witnessing all the money for which I'd struggled and suffered in New York go up in the smoke of one of those cigarettes. Yet name calling resolves nothing. We were at an impasse.

Moreover, as in the past, Laura gave a public airing to what, in my view, was our own very private business. I was mortified to discover that she'd told Eleanor I had herpes. Laura must have made the revelation in such a way that no one could have suspected how low I felt to have this disease, because, if Eleanor, always the soul of tact, had realized, she would never have phoned me to discuss the matter.

And Eleanor wasn't the only recipient of this knowledge, nor was the mere fact of my herpes all that Laura made known. She actually told a large number of friends of her supposed heroism in marrying me and sticking it out.

She would spend hours on the phone with her mother, as well, to the point where I became convinced that she was looking for a way out of our marriage.

The hostility between us was so thick that I scarcely noticed Nancy's presence, which plainly had no significance one way or the other in our relationship. Our marriage was, of its own accord, accelerating alarmingly in its drop into oblivion, and a third party was irrelevant to its demise.

Every conversation between Laura and me, it seemed, evolved into an argument. We discussed plans to travel to Kansas City after her graduation in May. I really loved Boulder and wanted to remain there, but Laura preferred returning to Missouri, and I went along with her wishes.

My plan was to purchase a used car and to drive there. I had the opportunity to buy an Oldsmobile station wagon and was eager to acquire it fast — before the owner found another customer. A station wagon affords a glorious family feeling, that I craved all through me. I figured that we could resell the auto in Kansas City and then, for getting around, use the one that Laura already owned.

Laura, however, had other ideas. Concerned over what might happen if the Olds broke down along the way, she preferred to rent a car from a national company. I pointed out that I was pretty skillful at auto repairs and that we had Triple "A" protection anyway. The primary difference between our positions was financial. Her plan would have cost approximately double mine, and she knew it, but she figured we could always fall back on her parents. I, however, wanted us to make it on our own. Resorting to their money would have negated all the work I'd done in New York. We fought, and we fought.

I even tried to convince her mother of the validity of my position, but she seemed unwilling to take sides and tried to change the subject. I remember her urging me to call her "Mom". I refused, wishing to reserve any maternal appellations for my own mother. At that point it occurred to me that perhaps she didn't know, after all, that I had herpes; if she had known, I reasoned, she would not have tried, by that suggestion, to get closer to me.

In the end, I gave a deposit on the car, never imagining how things were about to turn out.

During those arduous days Laura ran to one party after another — nearly always without me. I had no penchant for wild merry-making, and it upset me to see how far apart we had grown and how much she enjoyed an activity which, to me, was lacking in wholesomeness and dignity. She generally returned home drunk, and I imagined vividly her having exposed herself to ridicule by the other students.

I visualized myself walking out on her and hopping a bus to Denver, but found that I lacked the courage to do so.

One particular party, I attended with Laura and her friend Joan, whom I regarded as a bad influence on her. Joan routinely consumed an alarming amount of beer, frequently getting drunk. She had, for some time, been urging Laura to join her and had met with a high degree of success in getting her to assume a similar drinking pattern. At this party Laura ignored me completely — as if, I thought, she couldn't bear to be connected with someone stuffy enough to find drunkenness revolting.

As I witnessed her getting drunk and making a fool of herself, I felt contempt for her. I quietly urged her to leave, to no avail.

Then something interesting happened. As my eyes had once suddenly caught Laura's atop Mt. Sinai, they now caught those of another young woman, who had been observing my efforts. Without her saying a word to me, I knew that she understood how I felt. My pain and embarrassment showed clearly in my eyes. She hurt for me. Having this understanding and communication radiating from a complete stranger, with whom I had not exchanged one word, made me all the more aware of how far I was from Laura. With my own wife I had neither understanding nor communication, despite the use of many, many urgent, loud words.

Suddenly I knew it was the end. I had made a decision! And it was a real decision; it was a good decision; it was unquestionably in my interest, and it gave me direction and hope. I would leave Laura — perhaps that very night, or, at the latest, within the next few days. I would head back to New York.

By enlisting Joan's help, I managed to get Laura out and home. Once home, I announced to her that I was going to leave. In her drunkenness she shed many bitter tears, but, since she was verbalizing very little, it was impossible for me to know for how much of her crying my announcement was responsible. Because of her sorry condition that night, I decided that my departure would have to wait, but no more than the few days I'd promised myself.

Between the time I made my decision and the time I actually left, I passed through a fascinating mixture of feelings.

First, I felt frightened. I would be entering the unknown and giving up someone comfortable and familiar, as indeed Laura was, in spite of our differences. Furthermore, I obviously had to become involved with some sort of unpleasant legal proceedings in order to bring about the official termination of my marriage.

Second, I felt sorry for Laura. She was about to lose someone she loved. And surely she loved me, or she never would have married a jobless herpes victim who didn't like her shape or her clothing and who had no patience for whatever delights there might be in marijuana and alcohol.

Third, I was, despite my fear and compassion, absolutely ecstatic over what I was about to do. If God had handed me a choice between getting rid of herpes and getting rid of Laura, I'd have chosen the latter without a moment's hesitation.

Now, although I had made a decision, I had not broken free of all the habits acquired in nearly thirty years of indecisiveness. One of my habits consisted of persuading myself that a decision made by me really accrued to someone else, or resulted inevitably from natural circumstances, over which no person had any control. Thus I avoided feeling in any way responsible in case my decision brought about undesirable consequences. It wasn't even so much shunning responsibility as it was sparing myself the horrible sinking sensation that I could have avoided some disaster if only I had not taken this or that step.

Laura was someone I loved and didn't wish to hurt; I just didn't want to live with her anymore. I was going to play a game, first to make her want me out of her life, and then to cause her to think that she was achieving that goal. Whether from self-hatred, altruism, or ingrained passivity, I spent the next two days artfully confronting Laura with certain facts, principally that I no longer held the glamorous position of counselor, that I had an incurable, contagious disease, and that I was presently without an income. I wanted her to want me to leave.

I tried to be subtle about what I was doing, so that she would think that she had initiated the idea. In retrospect, I don't know how she could have caught on to my game because my method of ending our relationship was so wildly improbable — even to someone with a keener mind than hers.

At any rate, after two days of my making myself as disagreeable as possible, she asked me to go. Although she had seen my packed suitcase, I don't think she ever realized that I had already decided to leave. She was not accustomed to seeing me in a decision-making role, and, I believe, she regarded the packing as simply a childish display of anger, or possibly an attempt to get her to beg me to stay.

Meanwhile, on the second day of my obnoxiousness, an unrelated event occurred, which incongruously and with far-reaching consequences injected itself into our lives. Laura's grandfather died. The elderly man had been ailing, and his passing was hardly unexpected. It's safe to say, though, that Laura was more affected by the imminent termination of our marriage than by the loss of her grandfather. Yet she made plans to fly to Kansas City on the following day — this *after* asking me to leave. It was clear that she didn't need my shoulder to cry on, and I was glad for her self-reliance because I didn't wish anything to delay my departure.

Just before leaving, exactly fifteen days after my re-arrival in Boulder, I hugged Laura. People can't have spent time together and been close without retaining some poignant feelings for each other.

I gave a fleeting thought to the sore throat I was developing and to the rain outside. Then I turned and went out.

Despite these less-than-perfect conditions of my walk to the bus stop, I was deliriously happy. I couldn't believe such a wonderful thing was happening to me, and it seemed dazzlingly unreal until I boarded that bus to Denver.

I was a free man. I had no more ball and chain. I cannot remember a moment of greater happiness in my whole life. The people on the bus must have thought I was a trifle dim-witted, but I couldn't have cared less.

During the bus ride east from Denver, however, the soreness in my throat began to displace that elation as the focus of my awareness. There I was, at the beginning of a long ride, without a good night's sleep in sight.

We drove on and on, past the endless cornfields of Kansas, and, after one full sleepless night of them, I was feeling plain lousy.

Accordingly, I decided to break up my trip by staying in Kansas City until my condition improved.

Was I backing down on my decision? I wondered. Or was it just a coincidence that Laura was, at that moment, in Kansas City in connection with her grandfather's funeral? At the time, I told myself that Laura was still a friend and that, if the tables were turned, I'd welcome her into my home until she felt better. Besides, I reasoned, I was all alone, far away from anyone else I knew, and my funds did not allow me to spend freely for a doctor or a hotel room.

It was evening when I phoned Laura from the Greyhound terminal. She said she'd drive right over to pick me up.

Meanwhile, I waited nervously, my throat aching, my head pounding with every slight movement of my watering eyes, and the rest of my poor body begging to be horizontal.

During my wait two men started bothering me, making remarks about my suitcase, of which I gathered they had determined to relieve me. As bad as I felt, I handled them in a highly straightforward, amazingly effective, manner. Very simply, I threatened to kill them if they didn't leave me alone. My aggressiveness apparently surprised them, and they backed off.

Finally Laura came, dressed in black, and carrying hot soup and a sandwich for me. My initial reaction within myself was that she was treating me like a poverty-stricken object of charity. She didn't love me any more, I sensed. I bristled, though not visibly, I think.

Then she hit me with the news that her parents would not allow me in their house. This bolt of lightning drove deep into my psyche and made me want to do something wild — to show myself that I still had power and control. How dare Laura's family reject me! It was one thing for me to make Laura want me to leave, but it was quite different for her parents to judge me unworthy of entering their home.

My old friend Michael from Jerusalem had been living in Miami, Florida, for several months, and I had thought of visiting him during my stay in the States. Changing directions now would enable me to indulge my compulsion to rebel. My whole trip to America was a form of rebellion anyway, I recalled. So was my last departure from Kansas City. I couldn't force Laura's parents to take me in, and begging lay beneath my dignity. The only thing to do was to assert myself by changing directions, fighting the current. It was quite all right for me to feel like a piece of wood afloat wherever the sea might take me — that is, until my existence as a valued human being, with the power of choice, was threatened. Then I had to act. I was not obliged to go to New York. Maybe Michael would be just the comfort I needed — a young man of my age, an old friend.

With all kinds of mixed feelings welling up inside of me, I sat down with Laura and gratefully drank the soup.

Absolutely determined to keep my promise to myself, I told Laura that we were finished, even as friends, that there was certainly no hope for a life-long relationship of intimacy between us; and she said she agreed, but that didn't stop us both from feeling distressed over our separation.

If people and life were simple, I could have had one feeling at a time toward Laura, and she toward me. Although the ecstasy of love — which I never had for Laura in the first place — might well have turned to loathing, at least I would not have felt the wrenching pain I now knew. The fact is that life is anything but simple, and certainly my relationships had been filled with complexity. Various parts of me still loved various parts of her. It was my other parts that had just won the struggle to be free of her, and the rest of me yielded to them the right to that freedom.

And so, in the Greyhound bus station in Kansas City on that June night, two people held each other close and cried, each mourning the loss of the other and knowing that there was no alternative.

11 Michael, Frogs, and Eggs

Right after Laura left, I phoned Michael. He was very excited to hear from another lonely wolf in the forest that was America, and thrilled that I wished to visit him.

Within a few hours I boarded yet another bus, stoically resigned to traveling with my sore throat and related discomforts. Before arriving in Miami, I was to encounter one more ailment — new blisters. Of course I was anything but surprised. Allowing myself to become run down and worn out almost invited herpes to take over my body.

Michael picked me up at the bus terminal, and I spent nearly my whole first day at his apartment, sleeping. Afterwards, I sat down with this old friend, whom I had known well since high school days, and told him the whole story of my herpes and my marriage. The unfamiliar sensation of having a sympathetic listener, to whom I could tell everything, raised my spirits and warmed my heart, but it proved inadequate to counteract the generally depressing experience I was to have in Miami.

To begin with, the heat and humidity in southern Florida at that time of year produced in me such lethargy that it grew increasingly difficult to surge ahead in taking the steps necessary to make some sense out of my stay there and — need it be said? — out of my whole life.

Considerately, Michael had gone to the trouble of securing me a job. On the day following my arrival I commenced work for a tee-shirt company. Almost before I had had a chance to adjust to my bewilderment at finding myself in this most unexpected setting, the job ended for me because of currently insufficient business for the company.

Like everyone else to whom I'd ever gotten close, Michael had a dual effect on me. His thoughtfulness and concern were counterbalanced by what, in my opinion, were unwarranted expectations from his friendships. Soon after my arrival, he asked me to deposit some of my money, slightly under two hundred dollars, into his bank account. I didn't want my funds in someone else's account, and we argued at length over the advisability of this measure. It wasn't that I didn't trust him. I simply preferred to be entirely in control of my own resources, meager as they were. What annoyed me was not the suggestion, but his refusal to accept a negative reply, his stubborn insistence that his way was the only right way.

Of all the friends I'd ever had, Michael was the most intense, the most fascinating, the most determined. I admired certain aspects of his character, but found others very difficult to live with.

Michael had a job as a night guard in a home for elderly people, and worked part-time during the day, as well, in chauffeuring a wealthy senior citizen about town as she ran errands and visited friends. From years earlier I had noticed that Michael loved to come close to rich people. Although fascination with wealth had always left me feeling uncomfortable, it was Michael's night job which really disturbed me, especially on occasions when I would accompany him on guard duty, for lack of a better way to spend my time.

I used to think a great deal about the elderly people in that home. Being in southern Florida, a haven for immense numbers of the aged, they were, typically, far from family and friends, and, because of the deteriorating condition in which many found themselves, they had to depend on the owners of the home for many of the needs which, at an earlier stage of life, they'd handily provided for themselves. By contrast, the owners were at liberty to do pretty much as they wanted in dealing with them. The unpleasant odor that perpetually filled the air made me suspect strongly that even the most basic creature needs of the residents were not being adequately met, not to mention their craving for love, friendship, respect, and mental stimulation.

As I reflected on the universal desire for longevity, I grew obsessed with a kaleidoscopic vision of a lifetime of hard work, cruelly capped off by detention in a place like that. Does this fate or something else like it stand grimly waiting for each of us who is "blessed" with many years?

After a few nights with Michael at the home, I decided not to return. I could not change the situation, and forcing myself into it added to the dejection that was already a part of my life as a result of my own problems.

As far as a job of my own was concerned, I decided to seek work in a plant nursery since agriculture was my field. I had seen a number of likely nurseries in the vicinity and resolved to explore the possibilities.

Accordingly, I borrowed Michael's bike, and, although I was a decidedly poor bicyclist, I pedaled a number of miles on each of several days until I had succeeded in securing employment at a nursery. I guess I was lucky because I had no green card or Social Security number at the time.

My work consisted basically of spending eight hours a day under the hot sun, removing weeds, with the assistance of a young retarded man, who spent a great deal of his time in chasing after frogs. Our employers were two homosexual men who lived together nearby and wore conspicuous earrings.

As I labored in the debilitating heat, I sensed the current and recently-past events of my life to be set against an altogether surrealistic background. I recall believing, or perhaps only imagining, that the relentless sun was causing my hair to grow faster than usual. And, watching my companion run after the frogs, I asked myself how I could possibly be where I was, doing what I was doing, when a scant few weeks earlier I had been struggling with the insanity of Forty-Second Street. I didn't fully understand my feelings toward my nursery job.

One of my duties, it happened, was to carry potted plants out to people waiting in their cars. These people invariably tipped me for the service. I felt the acceptance of tips to be demeaning, but I soon learned to go along with the custom, particularly in view of the fact that these gratuities comprised a fat chunk of my total income.

For one reason or another I didn't enjoy having anyone see me on that job. Perhaps being seen would have strengthened the impression, even in my own eyes, that I belonged there, when, in fact, I felt disconcertingly alien to everything the job entailed.

During that long hot summer I maintained a businesslike contact with Laura so that we could get on with the matter of having our marriage annulled or getting divorced. Now, although Michael's and my respective schedules of working and sleeping prevented us from conversing a great deal, we did spend a considerable portion of what time we had in discussing what might be my best courses of action vis-à-vis my marriage. I appreciated his deep concern for my welfare, but resented some of his tactics.

On one occasion Laura had sent me a legal document to be signed and notarized. Michael was adamant in his admonition against my signing it. As for me, I wished to seek legal advice before deciding one way or the other.

With characteristic intensity and desperation at what he viewed as my stubbornness, he grabbed the document from me and actually tore it up! He, of course, saw himself as being the truest kind of friend — one who was prepared to risk severe rebuke and even abandonment in the interest of promoting my welfare, as judged by him.

As one might imagine, however, I was none too happy about the rending of Laura's document. In fact I threw a small table at Michael.

Not long afterwards, he phoned her, making some far-out threat about how my lawyer would drag her name through the mud if she gave me a hard time. In a letter that arrived from Laura several days after that call, she told of how she did not appreciate his threat and strongly suggested, with regard to the legalities, that we "keep it clean".

That life with Michael was far from dull was not entirely due to our numerous disputes. As I reflect on my summer with him, I feel grateful for his sincere interest in me, which is probably what enabled me to lose myself in my work, our conversations, and various happenings. Worthy of note is the fact that, after the herpes episode with which I'd arrived in Florida, I did not get blisters again until the end of the summer. Perhaps, if not for Michael's companionship and help, I would have brooded more deeply on my life situation. I truly believe that becoming absorbed in one's work, as opposed to idly brooding, can ward off various ailments, among them herpes.

To return to the more negative aspects of my stay, I must note that there was a frightening amount of violence in the neighborhood where I lived with Michael. We used to hear about murders that had been committed not far away. Particularly disquieting was the killing of a woman only a few blocks from us. In some ways the area was more dangerous than Forty-Second Street.

One day, as I rode Michael's bike along Biscayne Boulevard, someone threw an egg at me from an open white sports car and then sped away. The egg landed squarely on my shirt and caused me a mess of trouble when I went to launder the garment. This is not to mention the dreadful, violated feeling I had as I pedaled home, my shirt splattered with egg.

On the following day I was out riding Michael's bike again. This time a drunk driver in my vicinity crashed into a barrier. As pieces of his car flew toward me, I was sure I'd be killed. Although I lived to tell the tale, I began to think in terms of leaving Miami.

Amidst all the danger and general unpleasantness, Michael and I used to go on weekends to a singles' club — actually a glorified bar. He just wanted to meet girls and to have a good time. I did too, but mainly I wanted some diversion from "the slings and arrows of outrageous fortune".

Weekend after weekend I returned there with him although I did not find the kind of diversion I sought. At least no one was throwing eggs at me, and the place had air conditioning, something sadly malfunctioning in Michael's apartment.

Mainly what I found was one more set of people with whom I felt I didn't belong. Michael took these matters more in stride than I because he was not forever analyzing and philosophizing.

A song that I heard repeatedly in this bar was "Welcome to America." When one doesn't feel welcome or wanted or happy, a song that reflects the cheer of others just underlines one's own discontent.

Each weekend, as I looked around at the smiling young people, who were likewise looking around at each other, I observed that each one carried a drink, but I sensed that it was quick sex that they were really thinking of, not alcohol. How miserable and vulnerable they all seemed under the carefree façade. I wondered whether any of them shared my thoughts.

Once, I struck up a conversation with a girl, who asked me to buy her a drink. When I suggested that we walk out to the soda machine, she became visibly angered that I hadn't offered her an alcoholic beverage. I didn't have the money for what she wanted and saw nothing wrong with becoming acquainted over a soft drink. I should have known that there was a way to do things in this bar, and that, if you failed to act according to the expected mode of behavior, you simply did not belong. I had made the mistake of going to a place that was wrong for me; I was again on the outside looking in. It wasn't just a matter of not having adequate means, I reflected; probably I would have offered her soda anyway, just to vent my contempt for a system which frowned on spontaneity, honesty, and depth of character, in favor of a preordained outline of events, requiring a show of money, easy tolerance of alcohol, and shallow sex. Naturally I though of David. He was right again, it seemed.

One late summer night, there was an eclipse of the moon. Watching it from in the pool near Michael's apartment, I felt weird and uncomfortable. I hurried back, intending to shower and to retire for the night. During my shower I discovered blisters. My heart told me I would have to leave Miami soon. I would make another escape from pretty much the same things from which I seemed forever to be running away — blisters, heat, violence, shallowness.

I set California as my new destination and began making arrangements to head west.

12   *Trumpets, Strumpets, and Doctors*

Determined that my "California plan" should prove worthwhile, I prefaced my move with a phone call to the University of California in Davis, where, I remembered having heard in Israel, there was an excellent agricultural school. From this call I became convinced that the job and study opportunities in Davis were highly promising.

I bought a Greyhound ticket to Los Angeles, figuring to make my way north to Davis afterwards, perhaps by some other means. For now I'd be crossing the country with an open ticket, so that I could break up my trip in various enticing spots along the way.

The only stops I'd really thought much about making were New Orleans, because of its flavor and history, and Houston, because Michael had a second cousin, Rona, a neurologist there, who might be able to help me with my herpes and who could probably put me up.

Uneventfully my bus rolled through Florida, Alabama, and part of Mississippi.

Dozing peacefully, I was suddenly and rather violently, it seemed, shaken awake by a man who turned out to be an immigration official. He brusquely identified himself and his partner and, without a hint of graciousness, demanded to see my passport.

In the first few seconds of bewildered wakefulness, I was gripped by nearly incapacitating tension and fear. In having to summon up all my mental resources, almost instantaneously, at a time when mere yawning and stretching would have suited me better, I fumbled for my passport as

I doggedly confronted the question of why they had singled me out for interrogation. Why, indeed? I asked myself, noting dizzily that there were no other officials aboard and that these two were not questioning any other passengers. If only I had been awake when they had gotten on, I could have sensed what they were looking for, in time to prepare myself to deal with them.

I think they were surprised at my having presented them with a valid passport, an Israeli one at that. It struck me that they were looking for Iranians, in light of the recent hostage situation.

How had they known I was a foreigner? I was not dressed exotically, and they hadn't heard one word from me until *after* deciding to awaken me. Perhaps in a different part of the country, with a greater ethnic variety, I would not have stood out, I conjectured, but, where I was, a Caucasian with darker-than-average coloring apparently didn't stand a chance of passing for an American.

They summoned me off of the bus and grilled me further. Where was I headed? How long had I been in the United States? What was my profession? Toward the end it occurred to me that they had already convinced themselves of my status as an innocent traveler, but had to press further so as to avoid looking foolish at having chosen to interrogate me in the first place. When, at last, they released me, I climbed back aboard, visibly shaken, I'm sure.

As the bus continued on, the woman who had been sitting next to me all along asked me what had transpired. Telling her about my little ordeal provided me with a kind of catharsis; I vented feelings of hostility which I hadn't dared let out at the immigration authorities.

Later on, in the middle of the same day, we arrived in New Orleans.

I placed my belongings in a locker at the terminal and set out to see the sights — according to no particular plan.

I enjoyed the French Quarter immensely, tasting deeply of the history and mood all around me.

After some time of immersing myself in it I sat down by the Mississippi River and gazed out at the steamboats. My thoughts turned to Tom Sawyer. A certain sadness and pensiveness filled my world, to the extent that it would have been hard to imagine anyone there not feeling the same way. But there is sadness, and there is sadness. It can be beautiful, poignant, touching, devastating, overwhelming. As long as it doesn't connect to my own personal tragedies — and for a lengthy spell there it didn't — it envelops me with a deeply personal, unsurpassed serenity. All of New Orleans, it seemed, bore a unique, joyfully painful combination of sadness and nobility. As my attention turned to a man playing a trumpet near the water's edge, I was suddenly consumed by the other kind of sadness, of feeling lonely and far away from everything. I resented the intrusion of my personal unhappiness upon an otherwise vaguely pleasant pensiveness. The sensation of *déjà vu* then tugged at my mind, though I didn't know just why.

I next picked myself up and headed for Preservation Hall. The throngs of tourists there increased my discomfort with the heat and humidity. Watching the musicians, I noted that they were quite elderly, and I started comparing them to the residents at the home where Michael worked. The musicians were far more fortunate. Even when they died, I was told, there would be orchestras playing at their funerals.

As evening fell, I found myself once again walking through the streets of the French Quarter, where one could now see naked girls waving from windows. It fascinated and disturbed me how streets so noble and poetic during the day could change to something so cheap with the approach of night.

At some time during my little tour Cindy crossed my mind. I had been friendly with her at the university in Jerusalem. She lived in New Orleans, and the thought of seeing a familiar face propelled me into looking up her number and phoning her. She seemed very excited to hear from me, and I was quite pleased when she said she'd come to meet me.

Cindy arrived by car at about 9:00 p.m., and we spent the next four hours exploring more of the French Quarter and talking about what had gone on with our respective lives since Jerusalem.

At 1:00 in the morning, Cindy having invited me to spend the night, we pulled up in front of the house where she lived with her parents. She said she preferred me to wait outside while she went in. Suddenly I didn't like the looks of things. After my phone call Cindy probably had argued with her parents about having me spend the night and had left home in a huff, reasoning that, if she could show them that I was already on their doorstep, the *fait accompli* of my presence would constitute sufficient pressure to force them into allowing me to stay.

When Cindy came out, some ten minutes later, I discovered that my reasoning had been essentially correct, and that hers had not. My presence at their door notwithstanding, her parents would not allow me in. She felt embarrassed and disappointed.

But I felt worse. Rejection by Laura's parents and persecution by the immigration authorities were a trifle too fresh in my mind for me to take this rebuff lightly.

Although I questioned Cindy's judgment in extending me this invitation without first securing her parents' permission, I did not criticize her, nor did I feel angry at her either. I just left, not even asking for a ride to somewhere else.

I had no idea when I might be returning to New Orleans; yet I knew it would be better for me to leave town. I did not consider staying in a hotel, as I might have done if I had never thought of Cindy in the first place.

The problem then facing me was how, at that hour, to get from her house to the downtown area, where the bus terminal was located. By luck I was able to catch a local bus downtown, but even the closest station to the Greyhound terminal left me a hefty walk away from it.

As I walked along, I became aware that two men were following me. My heart started to pound. I quickly scooped up two stones from the ground, increased my pace, and played with the stones as loudly as I could, striking them against each other in the hope that my pursuers would think me more aggressive and less terrified than I was.

Somehow I arrived safely at the terminal, withdrew my belongings from the locker, and awaited a bus to Houston.

At about 4:00 a.m. a bus pulled out of New Orleans, with exhausted, rejected me on it.

In Houston this traveler, who was by then still more exhausted and depressed, took himself to Rona's home.

Rona, a prominent neurologist, was a divorcée, who lived in a big house with her five children. I had met her once before, in Israel, when she was visiting Michael's family. His branch of the family had escaped the Holocaust by leaving Europe for Israel, while hers had settled in the States.

Michael, thinking she might be able to assist me professionally with my herpes problems, had called her shortly before I left Miami.

In anticipation of my visit, Rona had arranged for me an appointment with a colleague who had had considerable experience with herpes patients. In telling me of the appointment, she tossed in the fact that he was a homosexual.

When I went to keep my appointment, it didn't take me long to see that he could be of no help to me. What's more, as we talked, he gestured constantly with his hands and made a great deal of unnecessary physical contact with me. I mentally prepared myself for the inevitable request that I let him examine me. When that request actually came, I turned him down on the grounds that I had no blisters then. For a moment I feared that he might press me further because of finding me more attractive without them. I was glad that he didn't.

Anything can happen in America, I thought.

That night I had a blind date. The young woman, a physician, was a friend of Rona's. I found her to be extremely serious and stable — so much so, that it was difficult for me to explain to her just what I was doing with my life, and, of course, our conversation grew rather strained. On the following day, when I phoned her, I could almost taste her lack of interest.

Looking back over my experiences of the past week, I could see how inferior I appeared in America.

It wasn't long before I was on a bus heading across Texas, New Mexico, Arizona, and California. As I rode, my thoughts about life had just the background they needed — a crazy man who laughed loudly throughout the entire journey, and a girl with swastikas tattooed on her arms, egging him on.

13 Alone in Davis

Eventually I arrived in Los Angeles. Deciding, on a whim, not to spend any time there, I continued northward to Davis.

My arrival in that town took place on a Saturday, one which reminded me of Saturdays in Jerusalem, only more so. In Jerusalem, at least the streets were not nearly emptied of people. Everything here, it seemed, was quiet, closed, and clean, even in the downtown area.

At a sidewalk café I spotted a girl eating alone and asked her a question about lodging. Her answer was simply, "I don't know."

Continuing on, I passed a Chinese restaurant, but chose not to go in.

I finally settled on a French café, which didn't look terribly expensive. As I sat back enjoying the quiet music, two girls smiled at me. I felt encouraged, inwardly jubilant. At last sunshine was radiating my way — after the long ride from Houston and Los Angeles. Nothing came of the smiling, but it was good to know the warmth of human acknowledgment.

My thoughts turned to Diane, a girl I'd befriended in Jerusalem and knew to be living now in Davis.

Having known Americans from all over because of my counseling job in Jerusalem, I seemed to have a friend of sorts in nearly every American stop I made. But, somehow, having contacts in these places didn't detract from my feelings of isolation. These people were involved in their own doings, and I existed only in the periphery of their lives.

En route from Texas I had phoned Diane. I now called her again, from the French café.

Within the hour she and her boyfriend came to pick me up. Both were very kind and pleasant, though somewhat reserved and noncommittal. The intensity of friendship no doubt being a relative thing, however, I felt myself tenderly embraced, as if by intimate friends, as I related to this pair the many interesting, if not so delightful, stories of my travels through their country. They did their best to be helpful to me as I acquainted them with my needs and hopes.

The couple accompanied me to purchase a bike, which they convinced me was essential to the way of life in Davis, not to mention to the pursuit of lodging and a job.

I didn't see much of them after that. They had fulfilled their obligation to this not-so-happy wanderer and were heading back to the bull's eye of their lives, from what I figured was an extremely peripheral point with me.

Anyway, I bought a bike for twenty-five dollars. With it I was able to travel around in search of a place to stay. Without much effort I secured myself a room in a big house, in which the adjacent room was occupied by another young guy.

I hadn't done badly for one day, but found myself a bit uneasy about my chances of soon obtaining satisfactory employment.

By luck I landed a gardening job quite early in my search, and, while it wasn't ideal in all respects, it suited my needs for the time being.

For the next month or so I biked around a lot, exploring the town, trying to make friends, and attempting to latch on to another job, which would be at once more lucrative and better suited to my qualifications. I did, after all, hold a master's degree in agriculture and found it a bit disturbing that my gardening job could have been performed as effectively by someone who hadn't invested the time, energy, and money that I had in my university education.

During this time I maintained a loose contact with Gilda, Jacob, Michael, Laura, and Rona, and, of course, with my parents as well. With all of them I formed lifelines which made my world a more familiar, comfortable place. As far as I knew, all except Jacob were aware of my herpes. Actually Jacob knew too, via a relative who maintained a casual relationship with Laura. Months later Jacob would let on to me that he'd known for some time, but, for the present, I took it for granted that he was completely in the dark.

Once, Rona called to let me know of the existence of a new drug, Acyclovir, which she said she'd be sending me shortly. This medicine promised to cut down greatly on the duration and severity of my herpes attacks.

As luck would have it, though, I was then in the midst of a fairly lengthy period of going without herpes. I had had no outbreak since leaving Miami two and a half months before.

I started to feel encouraged and optimistic about this state of affairs and grew even more so when I managed to get myself a job for the university doing research in plant genetics. This was no small accomplishment since there was a tremendous amount of competition for good jobs because of the students' willingness to accept extremely low wages.

Up to this point I had been working very hard and struggling to save some money. Moreover I had had no credit. Now my financial condition was much improved, and, what was even more important, I was engaged in work which I thoroughly enjoyed.

My last sexual contact had been with Laura in Boulder. As the course of my abstinence grew, I began to think in terms of re-entering the world of sexuality. My employment situation had aroused in me more optimism than I'd known in a long time. I felt hopeful and relaxed.

In addition, Laura had just gotten the divorce papers. I was single again. It's hard to say why, but, with or without herpes, I would not have felt comfortable engaging in sex while we were still legally married. Perhaps I would have done so if a good opportunity had arisen, but so far I had not felt altogether at liberty.

Now, however, I was free, relaxed, and relatively cheerful.

Around this time I chanced to meet a girl in the campus housing office. A wealthy law student, Lisa became a rather close friend of mine. As I grew to know her better, I came to see her as spoiled and selfish. She had a number of expensive new possessions without which I sometimes thought she could never have survived. Although I saw myself as quite the opposite, our friendship persisted.

One day she suggested we go to her apartment, and I strongly suspected why. With my resolve somewhat exceeding my desire, I went, but my predominant feeling was one of extreme tension.

At her apartment we started to kiss. Almost immediately she wanted to head for the bedroom. The suggestion and the anticipation, more than the kissing, aroused in me enormous sexual desire and excitement.

Beforehand I excused myself to visit the bathroom, where a thorough check revealed not a trace of my dreaded "friend" — only unmarred, beautiful skin, by the exposure of which I knew the ugly secret of its occasional victimization would not be disclosed. I now felt free to forge ahead and exchange some energy with Lisa.

Confidence surging through me, I followed her to the bedroom, where we made love. For me the experience was satisfying. As for Lisa, she was in rare form. Her sighs, her facial expression, and the relaxation of her body afterwards left no question but that she was totally content and invigorated in every way.

I got up and went to her bathroom to shower. Immediately I made the upsetting discovery that Lisa had her period — probably the tail end of it. This was something to which I was unaccustomed, and I began to feel disgusted and itchy. The presence of blood was, to my mind, unnatural and unaesthetic, and I couldn't shake the disturbing feeling it brought me. However, I made no mention of it to Lisa before leaving her apartment that evening.

In the morning my heart stopped; I had discovered new blisters.

Since I'd first gotten herpes the only girls to whom I'd made love were Laura and Lisa. This meant that Lisa was the first girl who had had sex with me without knowing of my condition.

One of the most difficult things I ever had to do was what I did then. Without allowing myself any time to plan what to say, I got on the phone with Lisa. Somehow the words came out. She had never heard of herpes, she said. Since her father was a physician, I suggested that she ask him about it. She became very upset, saying she didn't need such a problem at a time when she had to concentrate on her exams.

Of course I was horribly distressed and mortified by the whole business myself. I told her that, if she were to come down with herpes, I'd feel like committing suicide. I doubt that I could actually have done away with myself, but I wasn't trying to be melodramatic either. I truly felt horrible at what I might have done to her, and knowing that we'd have to wait perhaps another thirty-six hours before finding out one way or the other gave me the most helpless sensation imaginable.

On the following morning, after a fitful night, I got a call from Lisa. She had dialed me for the sole purpose of expressing the wish that I would die. The forty-eight-hour incubation period still not over, I was hardly in a position to justify the continuation of my life.

When, finally, two full days had elapsed, she had still not come down with anything. Needless to say, I was tremendously relieved. After four days she said she didn't want to hear from me ever again. I agreed, but suggested that she refresh her memory as to who had made overtures to whom on the night of our liaison. I also expressed the wish that she would some day get herpes from someone else.

If there had ever been the minutest doubt in my sureness that I'd never give anyone herpes, it was removed after that shattering experience. If I could come this close and not communicate that disease, I was surely doing something right.

After this devastating experience a terribly painful loneliness welled up in me. I saw myself as having no friends. My activities for a long time afterwards did not involve other people very much. Mostly I interacted with places and things. I grew to relate to myself as if I were two different people — so that I could have a friend.

During that lull in my life I bought a large Volkswagon station wagon, to which I became very attached. It was my only noteworthy property in America, and I came to think of it as my house.

I used to drive early in the morning through Sacramento, alongside the many fields, looking toward the Sierras, and very much enjoying the view.

Davis, I observed, was a curious sort of city. A typical campus town in some respects, it was unusually homogeneous in several ways. Nearly all the students pursued science or engineering courses. Everyone seemed to be good looking, healthy, and happy, and all rode bikes. Moreover a distinct competitiveness and seriousness of purpose permeated the atmosphere. In contrast to other American localities I'd seen, this one had only three bars, but seemingly innumerable fraternities and sororities, which played a big role in the life of the town.

After spending some time in Davis, I came to view it as a golden cage or a greenhouse. It was isolated and safe, but lacking in stimulation because everyone did the same thing. For my part, I discovered that, without friends, one had very little to do there beyond tending to one's studies and earning one's living.

There was no question but that I lacked friends. This lack was, no doubt, partially caused by my being considerably older than the average student there and feeling acutely aware of the age difference.

One day, in the campus housing office, I ran into a young Israeli student, Avram. We struck up a conversation and became good friends. I found out that he was working for his Ph.D. in engineering and was every bit as lonely as I.

In the months that followed our meeting, we biked around a lot together and discussed life in America and Israel. Early on in our friendship I found it gratifying to have stumbled into a job for Avram, one for which he was very grateful. Getting up at five in the morning to pick melons for four dollars an hour might not have been some people's idea of a great life, but it pleased him tremendously. He had not been looking for something permanent and found the extra money from this job exceedingly useful.

As satisfying as my friendship with Avram was, I still felt the effects of a devastating loneliness brought about by the nature of the community where I was living, the fact that I had a disease that profoundly affected my social relationships, and certain traits within my personality.

Though Davis was a pretty good place in many ways, I never found myself there because I didn't have the right company. It's not out of snobbery that I say this; I never looked down on the students of Davis. Rather, I say it because of my awareness, then and now, of the fact that my own approach to life, my own interests, and my own very private feelings and thoughts deviated from those of the composite Davis student sufficiently to render us incompatible.

It wasn't only my age, my indifference to fraternities, my herpes, my being a foreigner. In many little ways I was reminded of how removed I was from the center of things. During lunch break from work, for example, my companions talked incessantly about their pet cats. Quite often some workers even brought their cats in. For some inexplicable reason, these small, furry creatures invariably found their way to my lap. Not knowing what on earth to do with them, I felt embarrassed and uncomfortable. I would go through the motions of petting them and urging them down. Unfortunately they seemed to adore me and often failed to take my hint.

"Davis is not America," people used to say. But, America or not, it was not meeting my needs. I felt I was in the Dark Ages for all the stimulation I was getting.

I devoted increasing amounts of time to study and research because I felt more comfortable with my soul cloistered in academia. Having predominantly myself for company, I was forced to invest more in myself and to learn more about that strange, mysterious person I loved passionately, with total understanding, and yet yearned to love with more acceptance. I took good care of my body, eating well and exercising, knowing that good general health tended to keep herpes at bay.

I used to drive to Lake Tahoe. I didn't care at all for the main attractions there, the gambling and the shows, but the natural beauty of the lake and the mountains, as well as the clear, fresh air, made me think that Heaven itself must look like that.

At those times, my thoughts drifted to my parents, who'd never had a chance to enjoy a few days in a place like that. Oh, how I wished to have the finances to send for them — even for a short time. I used to phone them every weekend and try to share some of my more beautiful experiences with them. It was already February, 1982, nearly a year and a half since I'd seen them.

On a few occasions I drove to San Francisco. I would sit parked for hours, looking at the Golden Gate Bridge and everything around it. Hungrily I took in the ocean, the foghorns, and the sea gulls, as I'd done on my first visit there. The sight of the setting sun breaking on the ocean was overwhelming. All that I saw and heard merely provided a backdrop for the feelings I was having. I felt far from home and discovered myself experiencing an acute need for my family. I felt isolated from all my friends. In Davis I was in a vacuum.

During one of these deep communications with myself in San Francisco a strange, fascinating, stimulating idea took root and seemed to be rescuing me from stagnation. I would call Barbara. Maybe I'd just chat with her, or perhaps we could somehow meet. But no matter. I had something different to look forward to, even if it never materialized. My feelings at that point strongly resembled those I'd had upon first hatching the idea to come to the United States.

I didn't have a number for Barbara in Chicago and wasn't able to get it from the phone company. But it occurred to me that I might try her sister in Connecticut. With little difficulty I succeeded in reaching the sister and, through her, got Barbara's number.

When I phoned Barbara, she was astonished to hear from me. We stayed on for over an hour. There seemed some spark left of our former relationship, and she decided to travel to California to visit me.

After about a week and a half I went to the Greyhound bus station in Davis to meet her. Very excited and nervous, I worried about how I would look. I arranged and rearranged my hair seemingly countless times. I wondered how I'd feel seeing Barbara in a different setting. All the feelings that I thought had been laid to rest many months before rose to the surface as I paced the floor awaiting her bus.

When, finally, we laid eyes on each other, we both smiled broadly and hugged and kissed. Holding Barbara in my arms I could feel how warm and excited she was although we hadn't even left the bus terminal.

The first thing we did was to go for Häagen-Dazs ice cream. I hardly recall what we talked about. I think it was of no concern to either of us. We were once again communicating on a nonverbal level.

When we arrived at my house, the fellow from the adjacent room was there. Seeing lovely Barbara he gave me a knowing glance and a smile and quietly congratulated me. Even from our not-so-deep conversations he knew that I hadn't slept with a girl in some three months, my last partner being Lisa.

Of course Barbara and I both knew what we were going to do that night. It was going to be memorable because there was still something special between us.

Barbara had always transported me to the stars when we made love. But now I could see, I think more clearly than ever before, how I affected her.

As we prepared for the night, we reminisced about our days in Israel. We got to talking about our respective personal traits and the character of our relationship. I had always found her too strong, almost unfeminine. I felt inadequate in the face of what I viewed as my inability to keep up with her fast pace of living. On this occasion, maybe because of the changed setting, I was able to convey these feelings to her. She told me that she would welcome my being more assertive, that we didn't have to agree on everything.

We talked on about such matters for a while and gradually, spontaneously grew closer physically. It wasn't long before we were out of our clothing, in each other's embrace, and in the throes of passionate lovemaking. Barbara was an oasis for me; I could have sex freely and honestly with her, and I, at last, had someone to whom I could relate my profoundest feelings.

I think Barbara was a genius and a philosopher of great depth in matters of sex. She revealed to me that evening the most intimate feelings that she had always experienced during sex with me, and I could actually see these feelings take shape as we made love that night. Not merely a shallow young girl capable of removing her jeans impulsively in the bushes, she did what she did, that and all else sexual, for the very mature, lofty, and hedonistic purpose of deriving out of this otherwise gray and somber life all the glory possible via the sexual experience.

To lose yourself totally in interacting sexually with another human creature is a profound thing to do, and certainly this is what Barbara did. Having no inhibitions whatsoever, she repeatedly screamed out to me with joy, as if lost in another world. Though I always enjoyed myself enormously during sex with Barbara, I actually found myself envying her this time. Her pleasure was not of this earth.

I had, until then, taken for granted that a woman whose eyes were open during sex was probably bored stiff. To be carried away into the ecstasy of love-making involved the closing of the eyes.

Not so with Barbara. Her behavior transcended standard interpretation. Her eyes were wide open throughout. She was making love to *me*, the person and the body. Whether it was love she felt for me, or something on a lower plane, it was clearly for *me*. I was not just being used as a pleasure tool. Keeping her eyes open enabled her more intensely than ever she could have done otherwise to taste deeply the essence of me, and that was what she desired. Whenever my own eyes were open, I could see her drinking me in with hers. We would unite sexually and then separate, as if to hold onto the exquisitely mounting tension as long as possible. She had said that she needed to know my body intimately and passionately. She looked deeply into my eyes and scanned my face and kissed me. Then she ran her hands down along my body and followed with her lips. And all the while her eyes were open.

Usually during sex I was very much aware of my partner's body, what I was doing with it, and how I was reacting. With Barbara now, by contrast, I was more aware what *she* was feeling and how she reacted to me. The rest of the room did not exist for her. I don't think her eyes took in anything but me. My body felt like a shrine at which she worshipped. It was all very soothing to my wounded ego and shaky self-image.

Even at the moment of her coming, Barbara's eyes were still open. Her ecstasy was a spectacle to behold. Despite our attempts to prolong the pleasure, she came rather quickly. As with everything else, Barbara knew just how to extricate joy from life, and there was no waiting for it.

Afterwards I was compelled to go from the sublime to the ridiculous. That's how it is when you have herpes, and still more so when your partner does as well.

I fairly leaped into the shower and spent a notably lengthy time there. When I returned to Barbara, she asked why I'd taken so long. I just wanted to feel safe, I replied. She didn't seem pleased, but the subject was dropped as we again revived memories of our past relationship.

On the following day we drove south along California's famous Highway #1, all the while enjoying the spectacular view. We stopped to see Monterrey and Carmel, where, near a camping area, we stood together on a hill looking out over the ocean. Observing the dazzling sunset, we knew that we were truly sharing the experience.

We enjoyed a barbecued supper and prepared to camp out at a spot with a breathtaking view of Carmel below us.

During this time I devoted a lot of attention to my image. I was constantly thinking about the impression my conversation was making. I was forever fixing my hair and adjusting my clothing. I could not help but be aware of a tremendous tension between Barbara and me. Each of us seemed to by trying to outsmart the other. It was very obvious to both of us, and yet it went on. It's difficult to say why it did, because we weren't working at cross purposes. After a while we discussed this tension and the competition between us. I was sure that genuine behavior could only serve to benefit any relationship.

We collected branches and built a fire to keep ourselves warm. We lay down by it under a tree and continued talking. Very few people were around. We got closer and started kissing. I could feel how she was melting in my arms. Gradually we removed our garments and caressed each other's body, but I wouldn't have intercourse with her. She began screaming, as on the previous night, except that now it stemmed from frustration rather than satisfaction. I, myself, was tremendously excited by the experience — a beautiful girl making love to me in this splendid natural setting, by a crackling fire. Barbara begged me to continue, but I felt unsafe. Two consecutive days, with both parties' being herpes victims, would have been taking too much of a chance to suit me. As with last night's lengthy shower, Barbara was insulted.

We slept and awoke off and on during that night.

Around dawn I discovered that my driver's license and one hundred dollars were missing. A frantic search of the area actually turned them up, and I felt extremely happy; the new day seemed to be getting off on the right foot.

I became aware of the birds' chirping and the lapping of the waves. Barbara and I spent much time during the morning talking about life in general and our relationship in particular. After the past night's love-making, we felt freer to speak frankly.

Barbara stayed for two more days with me in California, in what could only be called an exceedingly intense meeting. We went horseback riding through the green hills, all the while conversing and enjoying the sunshine. This was Barbara's first time in that state, and she made no secret of having fallen in love with it. With beautiful, warm places like California, she wondered, how could anyone ever settle in the cold, gray Midwest?

When it came time for her to leave Davis, I drove her to the airport in Sacramento. She cried. Once again brave, strong Barbara actually cried. I didn't. It's hard to explain why I didn't. I had strong feelings about her, our relationship, and this visit, but the tears just didn't come.

After saying our final good-byes, I returned to my car, only to discover that I had been ticketed for parking in a prohibited zone. At least I had something to take my mind off of the emptiness which customarily accompanied my taking leave of someone close to me.

During February and March I worked a great deal in preparing a thesis which I hoped to use toward my Ph.D. I also spent a great deal of time chatting on the phone with Barbara in Illinois.

At this time I was getting herpes only every few months for about a week and was quite pleased with the increased interval. I was spending most of my time on my thesis and my job. Occasionally I would eat in the French café, where I relaxed and meditated. From time to time I struck up a light conversation there.

Once, I met a notably sweet, pleasant girl, whom I dated shortly afterwards. On this date I knew she wanted to sleep with me, but neither of us said a word on the subject. I had herpes at the time, as I did a few days later, when we had a second date. This time we were in a bar, and she suggested gently, but plainly, that we spend the night together. For no special reason, and with no real thought, I tried a new approach. I told her I couldn't, claiming a very personal secret as my reason. I should have known, and maybe I did know, and even hope, that she would beg to know what it was. She asked whether I was gay.

When I told her about my herpes, she was startled. Her friend's sister had it, she said, and she knew something of how sad it was.

On the following day she had an appointment with her psychiatrist and was scheduled to play hockey afterwards. She asked me to watch her play. I went, and we did see a little of each other after that.

But I grew to think that she had told some people about my herpes. I had no evidence that she had; it was just a hunch. Having herpes made it easy for me to think that people regarded me with disgust and had nothing to talk about except me, only in the most negative way, of course. I preferred to make myself scarce, or even to run off, when I thought people knew.

We gradually broke up. I didn't care a lot because I wasn't crazy about her.

One day at the French café, I sat eating crêpes, writing letters, and listening to recorded Édith Piaf music alternating with live music from a guitarist. During one of his breaks, we struck up a conversation, his wife joining us after a few minutes. It wasn't long before she made a very obvious pass at me. I didn't know how to respond. She was young, beautiful, sensual, and friendly, but incredibly lacking in the good sense to know that one just does not make a pass at another man directly under one's husband's nose. The husband, however, seemed oblivious to her actions and invited me for dinner some night at their house. We didn't set a date, but I gave them my phone number, and we promised to keep in touch.

A few days later the wife called to invite me over. I wasn't able to stay on the phone just then long enough to give her an answer, but I promised to get back to her. When I did, we somehow agreed that she would come visit me.

The next day, Friday, she arrived at the appointed time, in the middle of the afternoon. We sat out in the garden talking. Actually, what we were doing was having a talking match. It's fascinating how people's true verbal messages sometimes have nothing to do with the combined literal meanings of the words they use.

We started talking about Europe and the Near East. She had brought this topic up because it seemed likely to evoke flowing conversation since I was from the Near East. Little by little, as if she'd rehearsed carefully, she drew the conversation toward more personal topics. "Oh, you must be so lonely," she kept saying. She clearly wished to dwell on my social life, my loneliness, and other personal feelings of mine, as well as her own. I kept trying to swing the discussion back to world affairs and other more general matters. It was as if we were driving a car with dual controls, each steering fiercely in the opposite direction. As our car went zigzagging down the road, only a fool would have failed to realize that what we were really doing was arguing over whether we'd sleep together; but, of course, neither of the combatants could let on what both clearly saw was happening.

She, the irresistible force, was determined, and, so, she asked to see my bedroom. I, the immovable object, felt trapped, but I hadn't given up the fight yet. I first graciously offered to show her the living room, and then the bathroom. I knew that including my bedroom in the "tour" was unavoidable, but I hoped that dragging out getting to it would provide a big hint.

The first thing she did in my bedroom was sit on my bed. I felt uncomfortable as I studied her flashing eyes, soft blond hair, and shapely figure. She was truly desirable, and I wanted her. But I kept thinking about how horrible it would be if I gave herpes to both her and her husband. Also, I had visions of his coming after me with a shotgun. No, I would not give in to temptation. I offered to refill her cup with coffee. She declined.

At that moment my "housemate" passed by my open door. I cordially invited him to join us for coffee, and he did. She was very plainly insulted. Fifteen minutes later she got up and left, riding off on her bike.

I knew well by that time that, when I didn't have herpes, I couldn't communicate it to my partner and, therefore, not to any of her future partners. Yet I'd decided not to make love to her. Perhaps this was not the right decision. It makes me think, though, that most of humanity's decisions grow out of feelings, impulses, and hunches, rather than logical reasoning.

During that spring I made the interesting and useful discovery that, if I didn't enjoy having sex with a girl—that is, if she made me nervous, upset, or angry —, I got herpes. Maybe I would have been nervous making love to the guitarist's wife, lying there in bed with her while imagining myself staring into the barrel of a shotgun...

14 *Thinking East*

Summer arrived. I spent a large part of my time laboring on a project in the San Joaquin Valley, far to the south. This undertaking absorbed and pleased me and tended to take my mind off of my grievances with Davis, which I was trying to sum up and to bring into focus so that I could decide intelligently what course of action to take. When I got down to it, my work and academic situations were satisfactory, even promising. The sinking sensation that visited my stomach whenever I imagined myself spending the next few years in Davis resulted from the fact that the life of the mind and spirit for me lay stagnant. I didn't know where to turn and, therefore, began to immerse myself in my work so that I wouldn't have to struggle with an apparently insoluble problem. I wasn't even sure of what I actually wanted. Only my wishes were clear to me. I wished that a cure for herpes would drop out of the sky, accompanied by a loving wife and family, a charming place to live, a well-paying, pleasurable job, a Ph.D.

Wishing is easier than wanting because wanting must take reality into account, and reality frightened and eluded me. What was worse, it was so painful for me to face that I avoided dealing with it altogether.

One day during that summer I got a call from Eleanor. She and Kathy, she said, would be spending an extended weekend in a rented house in Morro Bay, not far west of my work site. They wanted to be sure to see me.

Excitement alternated with gnawing reminders of Laura. Uncertain that meeting Eleanor and Kathy would be wise, I knew, nevertheless, that I would accept their invitation.

They arranged to meet me at a restaurant near where I was working.

We planned to have lunch there and then to drive to their place.

Reaching the restaurant I was filled with enthusiasm as I anticipated seeing my old friends again. But even these happy feelings were marred by the realization that my life, since Jerusalem, seemed to be a whole series of emotionally stirring hellos and good-byes. I was conducting most of my relationships long distance, by phoning, writing, or just thinking.

The three of us were beaming when we first met at the restaurant. We exchanged hugs and kisses. I think I had become a master at the art of greeting dear friends.

During lunch they both told me how good I looked and expressed great pleasure at my having found a job that I really enjoyed. I'm sure I made similar remarks about their appearances and what they were doing with their lives, but I don't remember. When you feel unsure of where you're going and how you look and what people think of you and whether they know you have herpes, you become highly introspective and wrapped up in yourself. And, as if you didn't have enough to deal with in the way of a poor self-image, they silently bombard you with the accusation that you're conceited. Damn! People who are enveloped with warmth, approval, and genuine closeness can let go more readily and reach out. You have to be on the receiving end of positive feelings before you can get outside of yourself and empathize with others. The knowledge that you can make women's pulses race just by looking at them is an inadequate substitute, but it feels really wonderful when it's the only key you have to the experience of being wanted.

Over lunch we reminisced about our good times together in Jerusalem and Boulder, occasionally mentioning Laura, but not much. We drove to Morro Bay as I took in more of California's inspiring scenery. There were many high moments and much laughter as we relived all the experiences we'd shared.

In the evening they treated me to a delicious meal in a sensually memorable seafood restaurant, the kind that renders diners wistful by its proximity to the water.

The two women drank during the meal and continued when we returned to their house. As we all sang songs we'd learned together in Jerusalem, I became aware that they were both slightly drunk. Eleanor went off to sleep while Kathy and I sat up talking.

Kathy was a beautiful girl, tall and slim, with long, silky, blond hair. I didn't especially admire her after her "performance" with David in Boulder; I thought of our values as incompatible. However, I did like both her and her mother very much and wanted to continue our friendship.

I had never thought of Kathy romantically or sexually, either before or after my marriage to Laura, her best friend, but now I began to have vaguely uncomfortable stirrings. I sensed that she was coming on to me, and I took the bait. Eleanor was dead to the world, and her bed was separated from us anyway.

Kathy began teasing me until I was uncertain as to her intentions. I remembered Laura's telling me that Kathy used to enjoy teasing men, even leaving them cold at the last moment. I started to fear that she would do this to me. But, as she grew more passionate and yielding, my fears slowly vanished. It became clear that she wouldn't give up the pleasure of this lovemaking for whatever satisfaction a woman might derive from deliberately taking a man to a near climax and then abandoning him at a critical moment to maddening frustration.

When it was over, I knew Kathy had enjoyed herself immensely, although I thought I perceived annoyance at her having failed to frustrate me.

She smiled slyly up at me and said, "You see, I'm not fat like Laura."

Then it came to me. Kathy wasn't like Barbara, Lisa, Laura, or the guitarist's wife, who all wanted sex or love or closeness or ecstasy or some combination of those. Kathy's sex drive and response were normal enough, but her motive was something else. She wanted to hurt Laura by telling her that she had been intimate with me, and she wanted to hurt me by tantalizingly depriving me of her favors. But her scheme backfired when she found herself overcome by *my* favors. Then the best she could do to be hurtful to both Laura and me was to point out the contrast in mass between her own body and Laura's.

So much for my armchair analysis of Kathy's sexual motivations. The fact is that I no longer felt comfortable staying with Kathy and Eleanor. I decided to leave as soon as possible, which wasn't an awful lot sooner than I would have left had this disquieting little episode never occurred.

The mother and daughter drove me to the Greyhound terminal. Eleanor cried. With no knowledge of what had transpired on the previous night, she could think only of all the positive aspects of our meeting.

I bussed to San Francisco and, from there, proceeded to Davis, where I arrived early in the morning.

For the remainder of the summer I continued my work. In September I was officially accepted into the university's Ph.D. program for the coming January. Around this time I took stock of my financial situation and decided that I had saved enough money for a visit to Israel.

I then set about making plans, which included closing up things in Davis for a while and spending some time in New York before embarking for Israel. David having talked me into working for him until Christmas meant that my departure for Israel would be delayed for another three months, but the monetary rewards from laboring in a retail store during the Christmas shopping season would assuage my impatience to see my family.

A few nights before leaving for New York I got a call from Laura, who was in Kansas City. How I endured three hours of continual crying mystifies me to this day.

She had just broken up with her boyfriend and had heard from Eleanor that I was doing well in Davis. It occurred to me that Laura wished to revive our relationship. Was it my imagination that she wanted me only during successful periods of my life? What kind of love can be turned on and off? I asked myself, concluding that conditional love is a contradiction in terms. I was the same person whether I struggled for my next meal or whether I prospered. My heart and my soul were the same. People might feel either love or hatred for me, but only according to what they saw in my soul, not my pockets.

On the other hand, maybe I was misjudging Laura; our arguments had not especially centered about how much money I was making. It was difficult to know just what was on Laura's mind; people are so complex.

Since I was not particularly annoyed with her at that moment, I brought up the possibility of meeting. I might be passing through Kansas City on my way to New York, I said. I was curious to see her again although I knew nothing would ever work out between us. Somehow, despite having suggested the Kansas City meeting, I felt I'd never see her again, especially when she wondered aloud how her parents would react to my being there. We arranged that I would phone her a few days in advance of my arrival, but, as well as I knew my name, I knew that this meeting would not materialize.

The first lap of my bus journey east took me to Boulder, where I stayed with Eleanor and Kathy for a few days and where I was overcome by nostalgia.

From Boulder I made my promised phone call to Laura, who said she preferred not to see me. This time the rejection didn't hurt so much because I was sure it was coming, and I didn't care. I had the weird feeling that we would never see each other again. "You and your weird feelings," said Laura. But poke fun though she did, my weird feelings were always right. Laura and I never did see each other again.

I continued on to New York, my bus, perhaps symbolically, passing through Kansas City in a very uneventful manner.

As we rolled along, I met a young British woman, a most irreverent person, although she probably thought the same of me.

For many miles we sat together in the middle of the half empty bus as it made its way east through daylight and then through the dead of night. The other passengers, mostly sound asleep, it seemed, sat either away up in the front or in the rear by the restroom.

The girl put her hands on me, and I didn't resist. We became more intimate and actually achieved sexual union there.

What is intimacy? People refer to sexual intimacy. Yet nothing could have been less intimate than what happened between that girl and me. Neither of us had the remotest idea what the other was all about. For all I knew, she was a Nazi. Yet we engaged in a physical act which ideally accompanies and intensifies true intimacy — which is part and parcel of friendship, closeness, love, acceptance, and trust. These being highly elusive in the modern Western world, especially for someone in my situation, one often must settle for the kind of sex which merely provides fleeting physical relief. It's more difficult to have sex with someone to whom you feel close because then a sexual union causes each partner to leave with the other at least a little piece of that strange, beautiful entity known as the heart. Was I, who had so often complained of shallowness in others, now guilty of being shallow myself? At the risk of sounding defensive, I maintain that I was not. Of course the relationship, if one could seriously term it that, epitomized shallowness, but we mortals are not blessed with continuous availability of soul-satisfying relationships and situations. Sometimes one settles for mediocre or worse and then continues on in reverie.

As my English friend transferred to a bus which would take her to New Orleans, I continued my reverie en route to Manhattan, U.S.A.

It was mid-September when I arrived there and started working in David's Twenty-Ninth Street store. As before, I spent my nights sleeping in his apartment. From there I made occasional phone calls to my parents, Jacob, and others.

On two occasions I stayed overnight at Jacob's house. It was on one of these visits that he told me he'd known almost all along about my herpes. In a way, I was relieved.

One evening at about eight o'clock David and I were alone in the store, straightening it up, when a big, husky fellow he knew came in. David introduced me to this young man, Oswald, who had worked there for him in the recent past. Oswald expressed surprise that the store no longer sold mainly electronics, that we now specialized in clothing.

During this time there were two other men in the store, who didn't speak at all to Oswald or each other; they just browsed around. Yet I sensed, by their glances, that all three were together.

Oswald asked to see Lee jeans in his size, which I estimated to be 40. "Yeah, yeah," he said, agreeing with my estimate. I smiled, thinking his gruffness was put on. Ready to hunt up a pair of Lee jeans in size 40, I repeated the size, and he repeated the "Yeah, yeah."

It became increasingly clear that he was with the other two men. What disturbed me was that he didn't want us to know. Oswald looked decent enough, but I was growing uneasy.

Then he said "All right" to me and left, as did the other two. Apparently I was supposed to interpret "All right" to mean that he had lost interest in purchasing the jeans.

A half hour later the other two men, plus a third man, one I hadn't seen before, entered.

I smiled in their general direction and said, "You probably came to buy Lee jeans."

"Yes," said one of them, and, with that, pulled a gun on me.

In what must have been the next split second I saw the other two pull out guns, noted that there were customers nearby, as well as David and one of his girlfriends, and identified the three guns simply as two shotguns and one smaller gun.

One of the two men with the shotguns called out to us, "Don't move; it's a holdup! I'll shoot!"

Everything happened so fast that it seemed unreal.

The same man ordered us all to go toward the back of the store and to lie down on the floor there. As I turned to go back, I saw Oswald enter from the street. He told the others to kill David because David could identify him.

How can I describe my feelings at that moment, convinced that my old friend was about to be shot dead before my eyes?

Impulsively I screamed out, "Don't shoot! It's only money!"

The one doing most of the talking then put his shotgun to my head, saying, "Don't move!" He held it there as the others removed money from the cash register.

I kept thinking it would be over pretty soon, with me having passed to whatever lies beyond this life. I did not expect to survive this; I just wished it over.

Suddenly another employee came forward from the back room. Hearing the commotion, but not realizing what was happening, he started in to do what he apparently thought was breaking up a fight. The sight was incongruously comical. His entry on the scene, I feared, would be just the thing to trigger off the massacre of all of us.

This is it, I said to myself. I thought of my family.

And then, as suddenly and incomprehensibly as they'd come, they left — twelve thousand dollars richer. I couldn't believe I was still alive.

The confusion in my brain slowly dissipated. It crossed my mind that I would soon be visited by a herpes attack. Oh, there was no doubt of that.

But, as the days passed, herpes did not come. My intimate "friend" had learned to be considerate. *He* seemed to know that I had endured enough.

Within a few days, life in David's Twenty-Ninth Street store had returned to normal, whatever that was, and I continued working through October and November.

In early December I got a call from my mother that my father had just suffered a heart attack. I would not be staying with David until Christmas. Without a moment's delay, I picked myself up and left for Israel.

15 | Stronger than Death

As I sat back in the rear of the T.W.A. plane that took me from New York to Israel, a frenzy of thoughts passed in and out of my mind. It was difficult for me to grasp whatever significance lay in the fact that after a two-year absence I was returning to my family. Once again I studied the Alps and thought of Hanibal. I still had herpes. My illustrious career was perhaps just getting off the ground, but that was the best I could say of it.

I pictured my father, lying miles away in a hospital bed, possibly fighting for his life. I recalled two years earlier, seeing him lean dejectedly on the railing as I peered through the window of another plane. Perhaps this was even the same aircraft, and I was gazing through the same window. Since then, I guess I knew deep down that I would one day be winging my way east under these — or worse — circumstances.

My plane arrived in the middle of a dreary afternoon. Gilda and Adyli picked me up and drove me directly to the hospital. Seeing them after two years and smelling the citrus groves along the way made me feel as if I'd never left Israel.

Upon my arrival at the hospital, I was advised not to visit my father. The personnel explained that it would not be good for him, in his weakened state, to see me suddenly after two years. Even if my appearance there did not frighten him into thinking that the end was at hand, he would certainly become excited to the point of risking retrogression of his delicate condition.

I was, however, allowed to look at him through the window of his room. How strange I felt to be viewing him in this way, and how old he looked; time had moved faster for him than for the rest of us. Even my mother, who had nearly taken up residence by his bedside, and who looked wan and anguished, had not added on as many years as he.

Only the doctor provided me with a ray of hope. He was making satisfactory progress, she said, and would recover.

Afterwards I went home. "Home", in this case, was that old, familiar, beloved apartment inhabited by my mother, Adyli, now me, and soon, we prayed, my father. As I looked around, all manner of feeling descended upon me at once. Exhausted, dazed, and saddened, I was overcome by sentiment. The tears flowed freely that day. I cried and cried as perhaps never before. The sensation of being seized all at once by a great number of conflicting, powerful emotions overwhelmed me to a point where I ceased to be the master of my feelings, thoughts, and deeds. Gratefully and with massive relief I succumbed to the peace of relinquishing control, and cast aside the burden of keeping everything in.

Listening on my stereo to music from *La Bohème* and Charles Aznavour, I had an empty feeling as I kept reliving the airport scene with my father two years before.

After a few days the hospital allowed me into my father's room. His smile radiated warmth and joy at seeing me. Despite his condition I actually felt lucky — lucky for the opportunity to talk with this man. No one else was in the room, and we could be absolutely open, frank, and honest. Putting aside preoccupation with his health, my father spoke to me with the purest of love.

Having a vast array of stories from America made a good deal easier my task of breaking into what might otherwise have been a very strained conversation. He displayed a wide range of reactions to my stories. I was glad to be in a position to entertain and amuse him.

But I didn't want him to overdo things on our first meeting. I gently ended the visit by suggesting that he get some rest. Feeling tears about to well up in my eyes, I made a supreme effort to hold them back and to conceal my feelings.

As I walked down the hospital corridors, I pondered over how much he still encouraged me, as a father would encourage a son, despite the fact that I was already thirty years old and inclined to think that, if I had conducted my life differently, such bolstering would long ago have ceased to be necessary.

"Everything has a reason," he had said, "and every reason has a cause." Was this "cause" a person, a reason behind a reason, God? He must have been referring to his illness and mine. I knew I had reached a point in life where I would have to find meaning in my own affliction — real meaning, not just a way of coexisting. I would have to discover its advantages and analyze how my life would have been different without herpes.

My father spent the next three weeks in the hospital, with a chronic fever that stubbornly and mysteriously refused to clear up. It rained abundantly, and a damp chill filled the air. These gloomy weather conditions, typical of Israeli winters, formed an appropriate backdrop to the tension and worry we all went through.

I had notified the admissions office in Davis of my situation and had advised them not to expect me for my Ph.D. courses, which were then getting under way. In addition to there being no way for me to leave my father, Davis began to feel increasingly remote and unsatisfying. I no longer viewed my future in terms of its Ph.D. program.

I was still going through somewhat of a shock at being back in Israel, even without the stress that accompanies grave illness. Herpes was just around the corner, I was sure, but I didn't get it.

My father was released from the hospital and stayed at home for a few weeks. We would have been happy to have him there, but for the fact that we could plainly see him deteriorating. We stood by helplessly, not knowing precisely what was wrong with him or how to be of service. The fact that we couldn't let on to him how concerned we were intensified the pressure.

After a while my father asked us to readmit him to the hospital. At first we hesitated, but, after only a few days of considering his request, we decided to honor it. Certainly a hospital would provide a more suitable setting for his comfort and treatment.

It was already March, and the flowers were starting to bloom. As we drove him to the hospital that evening, we watched the sun set. The sight of the newly blooming flowers and the setting sun gave me the feeling of the beginning and the end simultaneously, but for my father I sensed only an end.

When he had gotten settled into a room, this time a ward, with a dozen other patients, I sat down beside his bed, and we talked.

He brought up his concern over the fact that neither Adyli nor I was married. He held my hand and said, "You need to find a partner." This time it was I who tried to encourage him. We were still young, I said; there was plenty of time.

All this while, I kept looking around. The room and the halls were filthy. There had been a doctors' strike going on for a month already, and medical care was minimal. Was the janitorial staff on strike too? I wondered. Socialized medicine has its advantages, but I wasn't then and there in the process of witnessing any.

Within an hour after checking my father in, I was speaking to the head of the department to try to get him moved from the ward to a private room. I thought he was being treated shabbily. My frustration grew as our apparent inability to change his pathetic situation became increasingly evident.

As he progressively deteriorated, I knew that he wouldn't last. Undoubtedly my father was as aware of that fact as we. "Death," he would say, "has many reasons, but there's only one death." I told him not to entertain such "foolish" ideas, but, of course, I realized there was nothing foolish about his thinking. His mind certainly had not lost any of its sharpness. My telling him his words were without foundation made about as much sense as it would have made for someone to tell me, at the height of the holdup, that I was silly to imagine I might be facing death.

From that time on, my family started spending whole days with him. All around the clock there was always at least one of us at his side. One day, as Gilda was leaving for home, she confided in me that she didn't expect to see him alive again. She needn't have bothered "informing" me of her feelings because all the good-byes she had just given our father made it quite clear to me, and probably to him as well, what she was thinking. He told me after she left that a person should say good-bye only once. There's nothing to cherish afterwards in the memory of excessive farewells.

During all this time the air was filled with preparations for Passover. Spring was in full bloom, and there was a feeling of renewal around us. My family, however, felt isolated, as if sealed off in a transparent glass bubble. Our extended family and friends behaved in a most supportive manner, but no one could eradicate our misery. They could share our suffering up to a point and bolster our morale, but, in fact, each one was able to leave us for a happier situation. We had no escape. There was the egocentric predicament in evidence again. With herpes I had been totally alone. Now I shared that "bubble" with my parents and sisters.

There soon came a time when we knew that my father had only a matter of hours to live. The various physicians on duty gave us conflicting, confusing stories. It was apparent that no one really knew much of anything, and the doctor in charge said plainly there was nothing she could do.

Shortly before dying my father said, "It's God's will." I held his hand, and we all stood by his bed when the moment of death arrived. We closed his eyes, kissed him, and cried. It was three o'clock on a Saturday morning. I looked at him again and again. He seemed to be at rest from suffering.

Somewhere in Jewish tradition it's said that only very good people die on Saturday, the Jewish Sabbath. It's also said that, if someone suffers before dying, that person's spirit goes directly to heaven.

My father's death seemed so natural. We stayed with him for a while, experiencing our own very private grief. Then we notified the hospital personnel.

As we walked out of the building, the sun was just rising. We drove home in a strange, sad silence. The birds were chirping. Life goes on.

On the following day we buried my father. The funeral was attended by many hundreds of people — relatives, friends, and clients.

In Israel, in the strictest Jewish tradition, the deceased is not placed in a coffin, but wrapped in a shroud and carried on a stretcher. At some point during the proceedings I put my hand on my father's head in a gesture of affection, respect, and farewell. At the appropriate time I recited the *kaddish* (the prayer for the dead) loudly. I removed the *tallit* (prayer shawl) from over the shroud and wept bitterly. Somewhat later, as the soil was shoveled into the grave, I looked at him and felt the keenest imaginable awareness that I'd never see him again. Afterwards we left the grave. The living go on with their lives, while the dead no longer shoulder life's burdens or taste its sweets.

At home my family began the *shiva*, the seven-day period of mourning. Despite the throngs of people in and out all day, little things around the house gave me stabbing reminders of my father, as if his presence hovered over our apartment. Feeling enormous emptiness, I realized that living through this death was the most difficult experience I'd ever had.

Curiously my herpes continued to behave considerately. I did not get it again for another four or five weeks. When it did come, I went to a doctor I knew; I heard he had recently done relevant research. He offered me some pills which were commonly used for eczema, saying that, with the drug in them, my blisters should disappear in three days. I saw that he was right. However, I began to be bothered by various side effects, among them dizziness and heart palpitations.

Around this time I was called to the army, where I ran into old friends whom I hadn't seen in three years. We were happy to be together again, and I enjoyed telling them of my experiences in America, but found the "recital" rather taxing because I had to fight to conceal the side effects of my pills. I didn't want the army to know about either them or the herpes itself, although I was a bit afraid to operate delicate communications instruments while under the "influence".

At this time my unit was in direct communication with other sections in Lebanon. I felt fortunate not to be in the front lines of conflict against the terrorist organizations. Having heard about fellows I knew who had been killed and a close friend who had lost his eyes gave me second thoughts about how serious my herpes was, despite the big problems that it occasionally posed for me.

I remembered my father's saying, "In everything bad there is something good." I felt a surge of happiness run through me as I considered the benefits I had derived and would continue to derive from my herpes. On the light side I had a tremendously effective, inoffensive way of freeing myself of unwanted women who came too close. More seriously, I had done a great deal of traveling for the first time in my life, and I had come to take better care of my body than ever before, paying close attention to diet, exercise, and rest.

Probably most beneficial of all was the perspective I had gained on life. Life grew more dear to me, pleasure more sweet. I tasted the suffering of others more keenly and, so, evolved into a more sympathetic friend. Having delved deeply into my own weaknesses, I became more accepting of the frailties of others.

Life may not yet have brought me all the happiness I could stand, but the sorrow it visited upon me has unquestionably been sufficient to show me the difference.

Epilogue

It's May 14, 1984, just four years since I got herpes. I'm back in the bushes — the memorable bushes on the campus in Jerusalem. Only a few feet away from the spot where Barbara and I made love, I'm sitting on a bench which is almost entirely hidden from view, although the bushes do not grow as thick as they used to. The air is fresh and sweet, and the birds are chirping. The midday sun shines brightly on the happy college students who walk the grounds and sit on the grass, talking or listening to a singing guitarist. How optimistic they all seem, how full of life, and how sure of themselves.

Suddenly here I am alone. I am face to face with myself and my odyssey of the last four years. Herpes has not conquered me. Ninety percent of the time I don't have blisters, and, when I don't, I'm just like everybody else. When I do have them, for a week or so now about every seven months, I manage to conduct my life pretty much as usual. The condition is not nearly as debilitating as many another illness.

The difference with herpes is that it's sexual. I'm haunted by the feeling that people who shouldn't know of my condition do, and that those who do try to avoid me. It makes no practical difference whether they really think or feel as I suspect they do; the fact that I hold these suspicions determines very effectively the feelings I have toward myself.

There are countless people walking around with oral herpes. They break out in ugly fever sores — usually after a severe cold, when resistance is low. Unless they go about in ski masks or retreat temporarily from the world, their sores stand out conspicuously to announce to others what they have. But no one seems to think a great deal about this kind of herpes. People don't speak of it in hushed tones, and they accept, as a matter of course, that those who are so afflicted will avoid kissing, sharing drinking cups, and the like, until the sore has disappeared.

In my situation the blisters do not show because I am part of a clothed society, and I do not share the kissing and drinking concerns of people with oral herpes.

But at that point my advantages cease — for two reasons, I believe. First, the general public seems to think of those with genital herpes as sexual lepers. They falsely imagine us as doomed to choosing between celibacy and contamination of every sex partner we have.

Second, we are forced into a moral dilemma faced by few others: to tell or not to tell prospective lovers. Obviously, if not for the existence of the first reason, there would be no purpose in withholding the fact of herpes. But, as things stand now, if I mention that fact, I risk the unfair and unnecessary curtailment of my sex life. If I don't, I risk being accused later of having dealt dishonestly. It disturbs me that I should be regarded as dishonest for concealing information which can in no way harm my partner. Would she be dishonest for not, beforehand, making it a point to tell me that she occasionally comes down with a viral infection which causes her a fever and all sorts of aches and pains? I don't feel like catching that, as I might well if we made love while she had it. Herpes, also, is a transitory viral infection, which would be regarded as casually as any other if people had more knowledge of it.

Oh, bitterest of sweets, the sights of this campus! The tears flow freely inside of my heart as I behold the panorama that is life. Life is like a circle because we keep returning, but each time, something is lost, to be retrieved only in the dreams that visit us in our most reflective moods of the present.

I feel I've come to the right place; I'm back at the source. A new generation peoples the university; yet I feel I belong to this place, this dear, familiar place which I used to love. I am not, though, the same person who studied and worked here. I have grown in many ways, and I feel older. This setting is the source of many of my troubles. My ill-fated, empty relationship with Laura was born here, as was the disease which altered the course of my life.

The people I related to here in Jerusalem have been scattered by time and fate.

I ran into Ruth not long ago. She's married and is still living in Israel. She seems content with life and appears to bear me no grudge.

Laura has remarried and is still living in Kansas City. At the time of her marriage, she sent me a letter to let me know, making sure to inform me that her new husband treated her far better than I. Ignoring the dig, I sent back a note congratulating her on her marriage and wishing her well.